Toxic Trigger-point

Shandra Higheagle Mystery
Book 13

Paty Jager

Windtree Press
Hillsboro, Oregon

This is a work of fiction, Names, characters, places, and incidents either are the product of the author's imagination or are used fictitiously, and any resemblance to actual persons living or dead, business establishments, events, or locales, is entirely coincidental.

TOXIC TRIGGER-POINT

Copyright © 2019 Patricia Jager

Contact Information: info@windtreepress.com

Windtree Press
Hillsboro, Oregon
http://windtreepress.com

Cover Art by Christina Keerins

Published in the United States of America

ISBN 978-1-950387-61-8

Also available in ebook.

Shandra Higheagle Mystery Books

Double Duplicity

Tarnished Remains

Deadly Aim

Murderous Secrets

Killer Descent

Reservation Revenge

Yuletide Slaying

Fatal Fall

Haunting Corpse

Artful Murder

Dangerous Dance

Homicide Hideaway

Special Thanks to:

Judy Melinek, M.D.

Crime Scene Writers Yahoo Group

And my oldest daughter for her eye for detail.

Chapter One

The hushed sounds in the Huckleberry Lodge Spa didn't evoke a sense of tranquility. Shandra Higheagle Greer closed her eyes and tried to float on a cloud of relaxation. But the soft rustlings, padded footsteps, and murmuring she heard only made her inquisitive mind wonder who was walking in the hall and who was talking. Rationally, she knew the fake waterfall and new age music were to drown out her thoughts and tension. However, she preferred the real sounds of wind humming through the branches of trees and birds chirping.

"Valerie is ready for you, Shandra."

She opened her eyes and smiled at the young woman who kept the towels and robes stocked, while inconspicuously taking away the used items. "Thank you, Mindy." Shandra stood, placing the magazine that had lain idle in her lap on a table and tossed the empty cup, that had held cucumber infused water, in the trash.

"Same room as usual?"

"Yes," Mindy said before disappearing through the door of the relaxation room.

Shandra walked down the hall to the three rooms used for massages. She came to the spa every three months and always had Valerie for her masseuse. The woman knew where to find the knots that leaning over a pottery wheel caused.

She put her hand on the latch of the middle door and pushed. With one foot in the room, Shandra registered it wasn't empty. Soft music floated through the herbal scented air. Lights like flickering candles barely lit the interior. A woman was face down on the massage table.

"Excuse me," Shandra mumbled and stepped out, closing the door. She was positive Valerie's room was the middle door. She'd been coming here for the last three years, ever since Sydney Doring added the spa onto the lodge.

Not wanting to walk in on anyone else, she stood in the hallway by the door and waited for her favorite masseuse.

Five minutes later, Valerie Howe, a woman in her forties who worked at the spa to support herself and her daughter, hurried down the hall. "Why are you standing out here?" She put her hand on the door latch.

"There's already someone in there," Shandra said.

Valerie studied her. "There shouldn't be. My last client left over two hours ago." She shoved the door open.

The woman on the table didn't even flinch at the sound of the door opening.

"Excuse me. You're in the wrong room. I have a

client." Valerie walked up to the woman and touched her bare shoulder.

Not a sound or a movement.

"Is she asleep?" Shandra whispered.

"Ma'am, you need to wake up and—" Valerie grabbed the woman's arm and dropped it. White marks appeared on the skin where Valerie's fingers had touched her. "I think…I think she's dead." Valerie stepped back.

Shandra took Valerie by the arm and led her out of the room. "Could you tell who she is?"

"No." Valerie's hands were visibly shaking as she rubbed the one she'd grabbed the arm with against her thigh as if trying to rid it of anything she might have picked up.

"Go call nine-one-one and report an unusual death. I'll stay here so no one goes in the room." Shandra wished she was in more than a robe and underwear and that her phone wasn't locked away in a locker with her clothing. Having been at crime scenes with her husband, a detective with the Weippe County Sheriff's office, she knew no one should go in or out until it was sealed off by law enforcement.

"What do I say?" Valerie's gaze was on the door.

"Tell them someone died on a massage table. Go." She gave her friend a nudge toward the reception area of the spa.

Once Valerie hurried down the hall, Shandra walked to the two doors on either side to listen and try to discern if anyone occupied the rooms. The one on the right had music playing and the faint murmur of a voice. Apparently, there was a massage happening in that room. The room to the left was silent. She eased the door open. It was empty.

She studied the room. Two cups of water sat on the small counter that housed the hot towel cabinet. The scent lingering in the room wasn't of the typical herbal aroma. It was musky and sharp like perfume. Closing the door, she made a mental note to tell Ryan about this room.

Valerie returned. "The Huckleberry Police are sending an officer and the Medical Examiner."

Shandra nodded. Dr. Porter, Alex, as she'd started thinking of him since her friend Miranda married the doctor, was the local medical examiner. However, his looking at the body usually didn't find evidence. He was the medical examiner by default. Being the only local physician, he was called to all deaths to record the person was expired. The bodies were then sent on to the State Crime lab in Coeur d'Alene.

"Who do you think it is?" Valerie whispered.

"I don't know without seeing the face. You said your last client left two hours ago, what were you doing until my appointment?"

The woman nodded. "I like to schedule that long in between massage clients to let my hands rest. I had lunch and did a facial."

"Did you see anyone in the hallway?" Shandra stared at the door. "I heard clothing rustling and voices while I sat in the lounge area."

"It could have been Laurie's client. We schedule in between one another so the people don't run into each other."

Shandra wasn't sure if that was considerate or if there were people who came here who didn't want to be seen. Why wouldn't they want to be seen at a spa? That had her thoughts tumbling around. Ryan said she had an overactive imagination. Right now, it was conjuring up all sorts of illegal activities at the spa.

Heavy footsteps and the creak of leather approached. She looked up and groaned. It would have been nice if her husband had been the first on the scene.

"I should have known you'd be in the middle of a suspicious death," Huckleberry Police Officer Blane said, striding down the hall toward Shandra.

Just what she needed, the officer who'd handcuffed her several years ago when she'd found a murdered gallery owner, and he'd been the first on the scene.

"I come here every three months. Leaning over a pottery wheel is hard on my back." Shandra stopped, realizing she didn't need to justify why she was at the spa to Officer Blane. "And we don't know it's a suspicious death."

The young man stared at her.

"She's in there." Shandra pointed to the closed door.

"Who is she?" Blane took out a notepad.

"I don't know. We found her face down and haven't touched anything." Shandra motioned to Valerie.

"And you are?" Blane asked.

"Valerie Howe. That's my room. The one I use to give massages." Her hand shook as she pushed a wayward lock of graying brown hair behind her ear.

"I see. You were massaging her when she died?" The young man's hand remained poised over his notepad.

"No! I was on a break. We, Shandra and I, went inside for her appointment and found the woman."

Valerie's eyes were round and wild looking.

"Can I take Valerie into the lounge and help her calm her nerves?" Shandra asked.

"As long as you both stay there." Blane slapped his notepad closed and turned to the door of the middle massage room.

Shandra didn't wait to get another look in the room. She escorted Valerie into the dimly lit waiting area and wondered why Mr. Doring, the lodge owner, or her friend and lodge manager, Meredith Gamble, weren't here to keep an eye on the investigation.

Chapter Two

Worry for his wife had Weippe County Detective Ryan Greer pressing his foot on the accelerator of his vehicle. The call of a dead body at the Huckleberry Spa had his mind spinning in all directions. He and Shandra had only been married three months, and it sounded like she'd stumbled onto another body.

At least he hoped she'd stumbled onto a body and the body in question wasn't hers. He'd tried to call her as soon as he'd received the call about a body at the spa. She'd told him that morning as he'd left for work she'd planned a massage today.

His heart raced as he swung into the Huckleberry Lodge parking area and slammed his vehicle into park in front of the entrance to the large log establishment.

Meredith Gamble, Shandra's friend and the lodge's manager, met him at the doors. "I can't believe this happened."

"Do you know who the woman is?" he asked,

having already heard from the Huckleberry chief of police that the victim was a woman.

"No. Shandra and Valerie found her."

His strides shortened, knowing it wasn't his wife. "How did they find her?"

"They entered Valerie's massage room, and found the woman face down on the table." Ms. Gamble shuddered. "I wouldn't want to find a person like that."

They walked through the door to the spa. A woman in her twenties and a man in his forties stood behind the counter. "I want the two of you to remain here until I can talk to you."

They both glanced at Ms. Gamble before nodding.

"You'll have to go through the men's side, while I go through the women's," Ms. Gamble said.

Ryan stared at the woman. "I suggest you ask anyone in the spa area to get dressed and wait out here for questioning. I don't think Maxwell Treat will want to worry about upsetting anyone when he comes to collect the body."

The lodge manager's face brightened in color. "Chad and Grace, go make sure all the clients get dressed and sit out here until the police can question them."

The two took off; Chad through the door marked Gentlemen, Grace through the door marked Ladies.

Ms. Gamble nodded to the door marked Gentlemen. "You can go through there. I'll meet you in the common area."

Ryan nodded and shoved the door open. Walking through the area with lockers, showers, and a sauna, he spotted Chad talking to two elderly gentlemen, sitting on a bench with towels wrapped around their lower bodies. Ryan continued through the men's area to a door marked "Common Area."

A push of the door and he stepped into a dimly lit area smelling a lot like his mother's yard mid-summer. Floral and earthy scents.

Ms. Gamble arrived at his side. "Down this way."

He followed her down the dimly lit hallway, passed a room with chairs and the sound of water trickling. The room with the body was easy to find. Officer Blane stood in front of the door with his arms crossed, glaring as if there were someone across from him, he was trying to intimidate.

"Blane, what do we have?" he asked, stopping in front of the officer.

"Your girl—I mean wife, found another body."

Ryan waved his hand. "I don't care about that. I want to know what we have in the room." He knew the young officer held a grudge against Shandra because she hadn't been the murderer he'd thought he'd caught on his first week as a Huckleberry Policeman.

"Female, Caucasian, can't tell her age, since she's face down, but from what I could see of her face, not sure that would help figure it out." He grimaced. "About all I could see were puffy lips."

Ms. Gamble shifted, moving farther down the hall from the room.

Ryan placed his backpack with his crime scene kit on the floor by the door. He pulled out latex gloves and his camera. "I'll take photos. Send Dr. Porter in when he arrives."

Shandra stepped out of the dimly lit room down the hall and motioned to him.

With his camera and gloves in his hands, Ryan

strode down the hall. "Are you okay?" he asked softly for her ears only.

She nodded. "You might want to look in the room to the left of where the body is. I peeked in and saw two glasses on the counter and some things looked out of place. Valerie said as far as she knew that room shouldn't have been used today because Louisa didn't work on Tuesdays."

"I'll have Blane keep an eye on it and check it out after." He peered into her eyes. "I need you and Valerie to wait here until I'm finished processing the crime scene."

"We'll be here."

He had a thought. "Could you ask Meredith to see which one of the clients isn't waiting for a deputy to interview them in the registration area?"

"I can do that. I wondered why she or Sidney weren't down here earlier."

"Meredith met me at the doors. I have to go." He spun around and walked back to the room with the body and entered. He started taking photos of the room and the body as it looked from the door. He moved closer with each click of the camera. A quick flick of the sheet over the body and he discovered she was completely naked. As if she'd entered and was waiting for the masseuse.

Ryan glanced at the robe hanging on the hook. He stuck a hand in the pockets and came up with a locker key. Which meant she had to be scheduled for a treatment of some kind to be allowed in this area of the spa. He put the key in an evidence bag and continued taking photos and bagging anything that looked out of place as evidence.

~*~

"I need to tell Meredith something," Shandra said to Valerie before ducking out into the hallway. She spotted her friend leaning against the wall opposite the treatment rooms, her eyes glued to the phone in her hands.

Officer Blane glared at her as she walked up to Meredith.

"Hi Meredith," Shandra said, drawing the women's attention from her phone.

"Hi Shandra," she smiled.

"Ryan asked me to ask you to check the people who were using the spa facilities and see who, besides me, isn't accounted for in the reception area."

Meredith nodded. "To find out who that poor woman is?"

"Yes. You don't happen to know if anyone was using Louisa's room today?" Shandra had a hunch that the room next door had something to do with the body.

"I'll ask Alice, the spa manager." Meredith tucked her phone into her blazer pocket and headed down the hallway.

Shandra shot a glance at Blane, who frowned, and she walked back to the lounge area.

Valerie's gaze jerked up from where she'd been staring at her hands. "Have they figured out who she is?"

"No. Not yet. Meredith is going to check appointments with the people who have gathered in the reception area." Shandra sat down in the chair next to her friend. "Can you think of anyone that looked like?"

Valerie shook her head, then stopped. "The hair was the same color as my cousin's."

Shandra sat up straight even though the supple leather chair cushioned her like a cloud. "Your cousin? Was she having a treatment?"

The woman's cheeks reddened. "She's had some hard times and has been struggling. I told her if she'd wait in here, I'd give her a massage after you."

"I was the only one in the lounge. When did you tell her to stay here and how did you get her back here?" Shandra's gut was telling her the body Ryan was collecting evidence from was Valerie's cousin.

"I ran into her during my lunch break. We talked, she told me about some of her troubles, and I offered to give her a free massage. I snuck her in through the employee's entrance. I figured it was my time after I finished with you and I could give my cousin a massage."

"What kind of trouble is she having?" Shandra had a feeling it would be good to learn this to help Ryan's investigation.

"You know, men. Specifically, one man. Who she just found out is married and not planning to leave his wife any time soon." Valerie glared.

From being one of Valerie's clients for three years, Shandra knew about Valerie's ups and downs when it came to men. It sounded like the men problems in their family were genetic.

"I see. Does she live in Huckleberry?"

Valerie shook her head. "No. That's why I was surprised to see her. She's staying here, at the lodge. Said she wanted to get away from the man and think."

"Where does she live?" Shandra felt strange asking questions as if the woman were still alive. But she didn't want to upset Valerie when she was freely giving her information Ryan would need.

"Las Vegas."

She studied her friend. "Did she come to Huckleberry to see you and your family?" It didn't make sense that she'd come here for any other reason.

"She just said she wanted to get away from her lover when she found out he was married and remembered her mom talking about this place." Valerie shrugged. "Her mom must have been talking to my mom because my family is all in Coeur d'Alene."

"Was she surprised to see you? In the lodge?"

"She tried to hide at first, like she didn't want me to see her. But when I suggested I'd give her a free massage, she couldn't get in here fast enough." Valerie shoved a lock of graying hair behind her ear. "She's nearly ten years younger than me and her mom wants her to settle down. I thought maybe I could get her to leave Vegas and find a nice man."

"Did you take her into Louisa's room to talk?" Shandra had to discover who had been in that room.

"No. I talked with her in the employee break room while everyone was getting ready for their one o'clock appointments. Then I took her to the changing room and told her to wait in here." Valerie slid to the edge of the chair and stood. "Want some water?"

"That sounds good." Shandra studied the woman as she walked over to the clear dispenser with cucumber slices vying for the surface of the water with the ice. She wasn't telling everything she knew. Or her cousin hadn't told her everything.

Valerie turned back to her with two cups of water. The woman's eyes were dull and her face wrinkled as if she were going to cry. "If Alice discovers I let Emma in here, I could get fired."

Shandra took the offered water, thinking that could be the least of Valerie's problems if the dead woman was her cousin.

Chapter Three

Ryan stepped back as Maxwell Treat, a friend and son of the local mortician, wheeled a gurney into the small room. Maxwell's shoulders were as broad as the doorway. He could have been a lineman for any professional football team, but he'd studied to be a mortician and taken over the family business.

"Someone get too aggressive with a massage?" Maxwell joked as he slapped his big hands together, making a loud noise in the small room.

"I don't know. You didn't happen to see Dr. Porter on your way here, did you?" The local doctor wasn't usually too busy to come to a suspicious death, but since marrying Miranda Aducci, he'd become harder and harder to find. If he didn't have patients, he was either locked in his lab behind the clinic trying to find a serum to keep him alive longer than his father and grandfather, or spending time with his wife. The male heirs of his family had unusual genetics that not only made them appear to be albinos, but it shortened their lives.

"I didn't see him, but his car was parked at his house." Maxwell winked. "I think they are trying to get pregnant before Ruthie and I."

Ryan shook his head and grinned. He and Shandra hoped their four friends who had married six to eight months before them would both get pregnant and then they'd be too busy to keep asking them when they were going to enlarge their family. Between their friends and his sisters and mother, he hoped it didn't happen for a while just to aggravate them all.

"He was called the same time I was." Ryan pulled out his phone and dialed the Porter's house number.

"The Porters," Miranda sang into the phone.

"Hi Miranda. This is Ryan. We need Alex at the spa at the lodge pronto." He didn't hide his irritation. When witnesses had to wait a long time to be questioned, they tended to visit among themselves and the answers to the questions he asked ended up sounding all the same.

"He's on his way. Should be there any minute."

Alex appeared at the end of the gurney. "What do we have?"

"He's here." Ryan ended the connection. "Female Caucasian. Not sure of age, hard to tell by the way she's laying."

Dr. Porter squeezed his slender body by the gurney and looked up at Maxwell. "Any chance you could move out of the way?"

The doctor's light complexion was the exact opposite of Maxwell's ebony one.

The mortician's white teeth gleamed as he smiled at the doctor. "Sorry Doc, I got here first and as you can see, there is limited room."

Alex glared at Maxwell and shoved by him, making his way to the victim's head. He pressed his fingers to the swollen neck and peered at Ryan. "She's dead. From the puffiness of her neck and the hives on her shoulder blades, I'd say she ate something that caused an allergic reaction." He put his doctor's bag down and motioned to the other two. "Let's roll her over."

Ryan glanced at Maxwell. The big man shrugged. It wasn't like the doctor to do more than pronounce a body dead.

Alex frowned at them. "Come on, help me turn her over."

They helped, making sure the sheet went with the body to cover her. The woman's lips and face were swollen so badly it would be hard to make an identification.

"I'd say she ingested something that she was allergic to, and it caused anaphylactic shock." The doctor pulled a paper out of his bag, made notations on it, and signed the bottom. "Here you go," he said, handing the paper to Maxwell.

"How long does it take a person to die from an allergic reaction?" Ryan asked.

"If they are highly allergic to whatever is ingested it can be a matter of minutes." Alex stared at the body. "But, it is strange that she was laying so peacefully on the table. I would have thought when her tongue started swelling and her throat closing, she would have tried to catch someone's attention for help."

"You think this could be a homicide?" Ryan had a feeling the body was posed on this table for a reason.

What he wasn't sure.

Alex shrugged. "An autopsy might tell you for sure. I would definitely see what she ingested and figure out if it was by accident or on purpose." He squeezed back by Maxwell and disappeared out the door.

"Need any help?" Ryan asked.

"I'm good," Maxwell said, unzipping the body bag. "Take her to Coeur d'Alene?"

"Straight to the state forensic lab." Ryan exited the room with all of the evidence he'd gathered and the photos.

Blane stood just outside the door. "Deputy Speaks is interviewing the people who were in the spa area during the time of the homicide."

Ryan studied the young officer. "How do you know it was a homicide? We haven't gathered all the evidence."

"Your wife is involved. It has to be a homicide." The officer's expression never wavered.

Shaking his head, Ryan walked to the room next door and opened the door. He agreed with Shandra's observation; something had happened in this room. After taking photos of the room from all angles, he bagged the two cups, a crumpled tissue and a plastic lid about an inch in diameter that lay under the edge of the cabinet. Everything that looked out of place was bagged.

Satisfied he'd gathered everything that might be of importance to the case as well as fingerprints from surfaces that may have been touched, he left the room.

"Put crime tape across both these doors," he told Blane and headed to the lounge to talk to Shandra and

Valerie.

~*~

Shandra looked up at the sound of approaching feet. She smiled at Ryan. His brow was wrinkled in thought as he walked into the dimly lit room.

He took a seat on the ottoman in front of her chair. "Tell me what you did and saw from the moment you entered the spa."

She reconstructed her arrival, changing, and waiting in this room. "I heard clothing rustling and voices, but Valerie says it was probably another client being ushered back to a room." She continued with how she'd opened the door and waited for Valerie. Knowing Ryan would be interested in Valerie's cousin, she added, "Valerie's cousin was supposed to be waiting in here, but I never saw another person."

Ryan shifted his attention to Valerie, "What's your cousin's name?"

"Emma Wickes, she was staying here, at the lodge," Valerie said, her voice wavering a bit.

Ryan prodded her some more and Valerie told him everything she'd told Shandra.

"And you hadn't run into her before today?" Ryan asked.

The sound of the gurney rolling back by sent shivers down Shandra's spine. How did Maxwell deal with death every day, she wondered? And he always had a smile on his face and time to help a friend.

"Our families never hung out together growing up. I saw Emma at weddings and funerals. That was about it. And most of the time, she didn't attend." Valerie frowned. "I thought it was odd she confided in me and took me up on the massage. She'd never really had much to do with our family." Valerie stood. "If that's all, I should go out and find out if I still have a job."

Ryan studied the woman. "Why wouldn't you have a job?"

"If Alice and Meredith checked the names on the list of clients today to the people who were ushered out of here, they're going to come up with a person and no appointment. If Emma tells them I snuck her in. I doubt they'll keep me on after that."

Ryan stood. "Why don't you show me to the women's lockers while Shandra gets dressed." He waved for them to leave the lounge area.

Valerie led them down the hall to the shower and locker room.

Shandra opened her locker, but lingered to see what Ryan did.

He pulled an evidence bag out of his backpack and dropped a key into his hand. He shoved the key into locker 39.

Valerie gasped. "That's the locker I gave Emma to put her things in." She spun to Shandra. "Is Emma the-the person we found?"

Ryan opened the locker door, pulled out a purse, and checked the driver's license in the wallet. "I'm afraid the body found in your massage room is your cousin." He held up the driver's license. The photo had a woman with the same color hair as Shandra had seen on the body lying face down on the table.

Chapter Four

Ryan didn't have evidence against Valerie to take her in for questioning, but he wasn't going to miss a chance to get her to speak voluntarily.

"Why did you sneak your cousin in here?" he asked as Shandra went into a cubicle to change.

Valerie stared at him. "Because she looked as if she could use a friend. We may not have seen much of each other over the years, but we were family. I've learned the hard way you should mend fences before it gets too late."

"What do you mean by mend fences?"

She rolled her eyes. "It's a figure of speech. Just our families have never been close. I thought that should change. Maybe I could persuade Emma to move closer to her family."

"You had no idea she was in Huckleberry or staying at the lodge until you ran into her today?" He found it hard to believe the victim wouldn't have reached out to a family member.

"I told you. I didn't know she was here until I saw her. And she hadn't acted like she wanted to be seen."

"Did she tell you the name of the man she was hiding from?" Ryan asked.

"No. Just he was married, and she was here trying to figure out what to do."

Shandra returned from changing. She shoved the robe she'd been wearing into a large wicker basket and faced the other woman. "Valerie, anything you can remember about the conversation might help Ryan."

"I've told you both everything I know. We didn't talk that long. I only had a half hour lunch break before I had to do a facial. Then I had a five-minute break.

"You didn't look into the lounge to see if your cousin was there?" Ryan asked.

Valerie stared at him. "I had five minutes. I used the restroom and hurried to give Shandra a massage."

"You didn't even glance in the lounge area?" Ryan persisted. It seemed to him, if she'd let someone into an area they shouldn't be, Valerie would have made sure no one saw her cousin.

"I saw Shandra standing at the door of my room and hurried to her."

"She did hurry down the hall toward me. I didn't know you did facials, too," Shandra said, glancing at him.

Ryan wasn't sure why his wife found this detail interesting.

"I was an esthetician before I became a masseuse. Having the two professions allows me to work full time here." Valerie brightened as she talked about her career choices. Then she sobered. "Hopefully, I'll still work here when management discovers I let in the woman who died on their premises."

Ms. Gamble strode into the changing room. "There you are. I've been looking for you. Every client and employee is accounted for." She handed two sheets of paper to Ryan.

"We know. The dead woman was brought in by Valerie," he said, shoving the papers into his backpack.

The lodge manager spun to face Valerie. "What is he talking about? You brought a dead woman into this spa?"

"She was my cousin. I ran into her in the lodge and after hearing why she was here, I told her, I'd give her a massage after my last client today." Valerie didn't look at Ms. Gamble. Her eyes were cast down to her white athletic shoes.

"How did you get her in here? No one at the registration desk said anything about you bringing in a relative?" The manager had her hands on her hips.

Shandra opened her mouth.

Ryan met her gaze and shook his head. He knew she wanted to take Valerie's side, but right now he needed facts. The best way to get them was to let people talk. Shandra wouldn't stay out of his case. The past had shown him if she believed in someone, she and her grandmother coming to her in dreams, couldn't let it go.

"I brought her in through the employee's entrance by the break room." Valerie finally looked at Ms. Gamble. "I'm sorry. I had no idea this would happen. I hadn't seen her in a long time. She reached out to me, something she'd never done. I just wanted to help her."

Ms. Gamble's stern expression wavered. "I'll have

to discuss this with Alice. What was your cousin's name?"

"Emma Wickes."

The manager's eyebrows rose. "She and another woman booked a suite for a week." She narrowed her eyes. "Are you sure you didn't know she was here? A week is a long time to not run into a family member in this small lodge."

Ryan jumped into the conversation. "What is the other woman's name and when did they arrive?"

"Bailey Ullrich. They've been here since Friday." Ms. Gamble scowled at Valerie. "And you didn't know she was here until today?"

"I swear. I didn't know she was here until I saw her this morning." Valerie's face had puckered up as if she were about to cry.

"Do you remember what room the two women booked?" Ryan asked.

Ms. Gamble shook her head. "But come with me, and I'll find out."

Ryan quickly bagged all the items in the locker and nodded for Shandra to follow him.

~*~

Shandra stood beside Ryan as he knocked on the door to the suite on the fourth floor of the lodge. She wondered at Valerie's cousin accepting a free massage when she could afford a suite.

The door opened. "Emma did you forget—" A woman close to forty if not a few years older, stood in the doorway. Her eyes widened before they became a wall of indifference. "How may I help you?"

"Are you Bailey Ullrich?" Ryan asked, showing his detective badge.

"I am. Why do you need to talk to me?" Her gaze landed on Shandra.

"I'm Weippe County Detective Ryan Greer and this is my wife, Shandra Higheagle."

The woman put on a bored face. "Are you soliciting the patrons of the lodge for donations to the police fund?"

Shandra felt Ryan bristle at the woman's insolence.

"I was told you and Emma Wickes are staying at the lodge together. I would like to know all you can tell me about her." Ryan pulled out his notepad.

The woman's eyes narrowed as she stared at the pad. "Why don't you ask her?"

"Because my wife and Miss Wicke's cousin found her on a massage table..."

"Cousin? What cousin—what do you mean found her?" The woman turned her dark eyes on Shandra. "What was she doing on a massage table? She told me she was going down to the lobby for a fancy coffee hours ago."

"I'm sorry to say, Emma Wickes is dead." Ryan stated it with little remorse.

Shandra stared at her husband. Why was he being so callous? Was it because this woman had been baiting him from the minute she saw his badge?

"That can't be." Ms. Ullrich backed away from the door and sat on the arm of a chair. "I didn't think she could get into trouble going down after a coffee."

"What do you mean get into trouble?" Ryan leaped on the woman's comment.

Shandra wondered at it as well. Ms. Ullrich acted as if she'd been telling the other woman what to do.

"Oh, you know, talking to strangers, pouring out

her soul to someone." The woman realized her slip.

"Was it because of the married man she'd left?" Shandra asked.

Ms. Ullrich's head whipped around so fast, Shandra heard her neck pop.

"What are you talking about?" The woman's gaze bore into Shandra.

"Emma told her cousin she'd come here to get over a married man who would never leave his wife." She stared back at the woman all innocence, hoping she was a good actress. There was no way she wanted this woman to think anything else had been said, because according to Valerie, it hadn't.

"Who is this cousin?" Ms. Ullrich glanced from Shandra to Ryan and back to Shandra.

"A friend." She didn't think the woman needed to know any more about Valerie.

"Why did you and Ms. Wickes really come here?" Ryan asked.

"You know why. Emma was trying to rid her mind of her lover." Ms. Ullrich stood, moving them toward the door. "I have to make some phone calls."

"To Emma's family?" Shandra asked.

The woman stared pointedly at Ryan. "That's his job."

Ryan stopped at the door. "I need you to leave the premises while I do a search."

Ms. Ullrich's jaw dropped for a second before she marched over to a cell phone on a table. She shoved it into her pant pocket and picked up a shoulder bag. "How long will you be?"

"Give me your number, and I'll call you when I finish." Ryan still had his notepad out.

"Call the desk when you're finished. I'll check in there." The woman disappeared out the door.

"Interesting woman," Shandra said.

"I bet you a dinner at Rigatoni's she was here keeping an eye on our victim." Ryan handed her a pair of latex gloves. "If you find anything interesting leave it lay so I can get a photograph."

Shandra nodded and headed for a bedroom. The first room was Ms. Ullrich's. The monotone clothes were neatly put away, not a scrap of paper or a book anywhere.

The second bedroom had to be Emma's. The clothing was vibrant colors and strewn about the room as if she couldn't decide what to wear. There were entertainment magazines, romance books, and chocolate wrappers dappled the dresser, wastebasket, and upholstered chair.

Digging through the empty suitcase and makeup bag, she found an epinephrine autoinjector.

"Ryan!" she called out, wondering if it might have a significance.

He walked into the room. "What did you find?"

She pointed to the open cosmetic bag. "A pen used by people who are deathly allergic to something."

Pulling out his camera, he took a photo of the bag, the contents, and the pen, after he'd put it on the dresser top. "Did you find anything else?"

"Not yet. With all the magazines and books, I would have thought I'd find a diary. She seems the type to have kept one." Shandra felt under the mattress on the bed and looked under the bed. Nothing. "Was there one in her purse?"

"I didn't see anything that looked like a diary."

Ryan glanced around. "You know what I don't see?"

Shandra did a scan. "Her phone. It wasn't in her purse was it?"

"No. Someone the victim's age would have a cell phone unless they were Amish." Ryan waved his hands. "Keep looking."

Shandra started running her hands through the clothes in the dresser drawers. A thought struck her. "What if the phone we saw Ms. Ullrich pick up was Emma's?"

Chapter Five

An hour after they'd started, Shandra followed Ryan out of the suite. As they walked to the elevator and descended to the first floor, Ryan was on his phone asking for background checks to be run on Emma Wickes and Bailey Ullrich.

Shandra led the way off the elevator and over to the registration desk. She scanned the lobby for Bailey but didn't see the woman.

"Leave a message for Ms. Ullrich, in room four-eighteen. She may return to her room," Ryan said to the clerk behind the registration desk before also scanning the lobby.

"What do you think she did with the phone?" Shandra asked, following Ryan to the door of the lodge restaurant.

He peeked in. "Either checked to see if there was any incriminating calls or messages or is hanging onto it to keep us from discovering who the man is Emma was running away from."

Shandra's stomach growled. It was after six which had been evident by the number of people seated at tables in the restaurant.

"Let's try the bar." Ryan backed away from the restaurant and led her down the hallway to the Slope, the bar inside the Lodge.

They walked inside, and at a table by herself, sat Bailey. She was using a stylus on the screen of her phone. Or at least, Shandra hoped it was her phone and not Emma's.

"Ms. Ullrich," Ryan sat down across the table from the woman, "if that is Emma Wickes', phone, you are tampering with evidence in a suspicious death."

The woman's head jerked up. She glared at Ryan. "This is my phone."

"Do you happen to know where Emma's phone might be? It wasn't with her belongings at the spa, and we didn't find it in the suite." Ryan continued to peer at the woman.

Shandra, who'd sat to the side of the table and closer to Bailey, glanced down at what the woman had been writing. It appeared to be an entry into a diary or date book.

11:30 Emma left room for coffee.

Noon I went looking for her.

1pm I started asking hotel staff if they'd seen Emma.

It appeared the woman had been more worried about Emma than she'd let on. But why the detailed account?

"Were you keeping tabs on Emma for someone?" Shandra asked.

The woman turned her glare on Shandra. "Why would you think I was keeping tabs on Emma?"

Shandra pointed to the screen on the phone in front of the woman.

Bailey quickly pushed a button, making the screen go away.

Shandra had scanned the top of the document and read the file name. Emma Wickes/Tabor Maxmillan. She'd fill Ryan in later.

"Where can we find Ms. Wickes' phone?" Ryan persisted.

"How should I know? We traveled here to vacation as friends, not each others keeper." Bailey stood. "Since you are down here hounding me, I take it I can go to my room now?"

Ryan nodded.

The woman strode out of the bar.

"She knows more than she's saying. Why didn't you ask her about allergies?" Shandra asked.

"I want to wait until we know for sure the victim had an allergic reaction and to what." Ryan stood. "Do you think Valerie is still here?"

Shandra shook her head. "I doubt it. She's a single mom and needs to get home to her daughter."

"Ask Meredith for Valerie's home phone number. I'll call and ask her about the allergy. That will give the forensic team something to look for."

Shandra stood. "You might want to find out who Tabor Maxmillan is. That was the name on the document Bailey was typing on when we sat down. And it was a time table of when Emma went missing from the suite."

"I saw it looked like a timetable of sorts." Ryan

pulled out his phone. "Why does the name Maxmillan make the hair on the back of my neck stand up?" he asked as Shandra walked away from the table and out of the bar.

If she hurried, she should be able to catch Meredith before she headed home.

~*~

Ryan scowled at the phone. What had Valerie's cousin been mixed up in? Tabor Maxmillan was a known money launderer and crook from Las Vegas.

"I have Valerie's phone number and address," Shandra said, walking up to the table he still occupied in the bar.

The waitress walked over with two chicken strip baskets and iced teas.

"This is why I married you," Shandra said. "You know how to take care of me."

Ryan sent her a smile and texted Deputy Speaks to join him in the bar. Once that task was finished, he pulled a basket toward him and started eating.

"After we eat, you can go home," he said, knowing he'd allowed her to help more than he should have, but ever since meeting the woman, she'd had an uncanny knack of solving murders with the help of dreams from her deceased grandmother.

"Are you going to call or drive out to talk to Valerie?" Shandra squeezed ketchup onto her fries. Her gaze rose.

He met her amber colored gaze, knowing she planned to go with him if he said he would see Valerie in person.

"I was thinking about going to her house."

Shandra's eyes lit up. "I think Valerie would feel

more comfortable if I were with you. After all, we both found the body." Shandra cringed. "Actually, I found it first when I opened the door and thought I'd gone in the wrong room."

"Ron, have a seat," Ryan said, stopping Shandra from saying more. He didn't want her comments to influence anything the deputy might have discovered while interviewing the other clients in the spa area.

The deputy glanced at their food wistfully.

When the waitress came over to see what Speaks wanted, Ryan told her to bring out another chicken basket. From experience he knew it was the fastest menu item.

"You remember my wife, Shandra," Ryan introduced the two even though they had met several times before.

"Shandra, I heard you found the body along with a Valerie Howe." Speaks took the soda he'd ordered, when the waitress arrived with it.

"We did. And I can tell you, I'm not so sure I'll be able to have a massage any time soon." Shandra shuddered and picked up a fry dripping with ketchup.

"What did you learn from the people you questioned?" Ryan asked, diverting the attention from his wife.

"Most of the people didn't even know why they'd been rousted out of the spa. Two elderly gentlemen said there was a man in street clothes who hurried through the spa."

"That would be me, when I arrived. I saw the two sitting on a bench B.S.ing." Ryan took a drink and asked, "Did you get all of their names?"

Speaks nodded and shoved his notepad across the

table to Ryan.

Skimming through the names, his finger stopped at Egan Trower. The name rang a bell. "Did this man say what he did or why he was here?"

The deputy spun the book around and flipped through the pages. "He was in the sauna, hoping someone wouldn't show for a massage. He said his occupation was salesman." Speaks glanced up from the book. "Mr. Trower acted like he knew the routine. He is either from our side or has been pulled in a lot and knows the drill."

The waitress arrived with Speaks' dinner. She placed it on the table. Ryan reached for his wallet, paying for all three meals.

When the woman left, he picked up his glass of iced tea. "Run all of them through the database. The Trower name sounds familiar." He glanced at Shandra. "Ready?"

She nodded, wiped her face, and stood.

"I'm going to interview the other witness then head home. Type up your notes as soon as possible." Ryan ignored Speaks raised eyebrows as he led his wife out of the bar. The county and state officers took pleasure in ribbing him that he'd caught more homicides since meeting his wife and that it appeared she was the detective in the family.

He shrugged it off with a laugh. He knew half of the homicides wouldn't have been solved without Shandra and her grandmother.

Chapter Six

Shandra stood on the porch beside Ryan. He'd had her follow him to Valerie's in her Jeep. That way they wouldn't have to go back to the lodge to retrieve it when they finished here.

Ryan knocked again.

Valerie lived in a one-story, smaller home in the neighborhood to the west of downtown Huckleberry. The homes were all modest, 1990s, three-bedroom homes on small lots.

"Finish your homework!" Valerie called over her shoulder as she opened the door. Her eyes widened at the sight of Ryan.

"Ms. Howe, I have some more questions about your cousin." Ryan said, drawing Shandra up beside him.

Shandra smiled at her friend. "It's something we need to know so the police know better how to classify her death."

Valerie stared at her and then Ryan. "What do you mean classify?" She backed into the small living room and plopped down on a ratty recliner.

Shandra moved to the couch. Ryan followed her, and they both sat.

"Do you know if Emma had any allergies?" Ryan asked.

The woman peered back and forth between them. "She's been deathly allergic to bee stings her whole life. She carries something to counteract the sting with her all the time."

Ryan nodded. "We found an epinephrine autoinjector in her room at the lodge. But I didn't notice anything in her purse. Do you know if she carried one in her purse?"

Valerie shook her head. "I wouldn't know what she does now. As kids, she had to carry something around when Aunt Betty wasn't with her." Her brow wrinkled as she stared at Shandra. "Did she die from a bee sting? How?"

"We don't know the cause, but it does appear she had an allergic reaction. Was she allergic to any foods?" Ryan drew Valerie's attention back to him.

Shandra understood her friend's concern. How on earth would a bee have gotten into the spa area? As far as she knew there weren't any doors that entered the area directly from outside.

"Foods? No." Valerie tapped a finger where her hand rested on the arm of the chair. "Except I remember once Aunt Betty asked my mom if the honey we had when they were visiting was raw." She leaned forward. "I guess the raw honey could have some bee venom in it. Emma nearly died twice from bee stings as a child. That's how bad her allergy was."

Shandra shuddered. She'd been stung by bees and wasps and only had minor discomfort for about twenty-four hours. She couldn't imagine living a life where you had to be afraid of the creature who helped pollinate the beautiful flowers around you.

"Does the spa use raw honey?" Ryan asked.

Valerie stared at him. "Oh God! Yes. It's believed to have healing qualities."

"What is it used for?" Ryan continued to write in the notepad he'd produced as soon as he sat on the couch.

"It's used for some facials. It's in the registration area to use in tea while clients are waiting. I think it's also in the breakroom for us to use in our drinks there." Valerie's eyes widened. "But Emma wouldn't have eaten any honey. She didn't even use the pasteurized honey from stores."

"We'll know if she ingested any after the forensic report," Ryan said. "Do you remember seeing anyone who shouldn't have been in the area of the breakroom or the massage rooms?"

Valerie closed her eyes. Her lips drew into her mouth as she tried to remember. Her lashes fluttered up. "I saw a man I've never seen before walking into the lounge when I left Emma. But he was probably a client waiting for his appointment." She waved a hand up and down. "He was dressed in a spa robe."

Ryan eased forward in his chair. "Can you describe him?"

She closed her eyes, again. "His head was about six inches from the top of the door. Tall. I couldn't tell with the robe he wore, if he was slender, but his legs looked like sticks, so I'd say he was thin."

"What color hair?" Ryan asked.

"Brown, I think. It was dim and he had a crewcut." Valerie stared at him. "Do you think she was killed on purpose? Not an accident?"

"We won't know anything until later." Ryan stood and motioned for Shandra to stand. "Thank you for answering more questions."

Shandra followed Ryan to the door, but turned back to Valerie. "If you think of anything or just want to talk, give me a call."

Valerie nodded. "Should I call her parents?"

Ryan faced her. "You haven't told your family?"

She shrugged. "I don't know what to say. I know she's dead, but what else can I tell them? Aunt Betty is going to want to know how. It's not like I can say a car accident or something like that."

"I'll contact them. Do you have their number? That would save me time." Ryan opened his notepad.

"Sure. Just a minute." Valerie retrieved a cell phone from the table by the recliner. She scrolled through and recited a phone number.

"Did you happen to see Emma with a cell phone?" Shandra asked, still wondering where the woman's phone could be.

"Yes. She had it in her hand when I called out to her when I first saw her." Valerie shoved her phone in her back pocket. "Why?"

"We can't—"

Ryan opened the door and pulled Shandra out before she could finish her sentence. "I'll be in touch with more questions," he said to Ms. Howe.

The door closed. Before he took a step, a tug on his

coat sleeve stopped him.

"Why did you stop me from telling her about not finding the phone?" Shandra asked.

"We don't need that bit of information to get around. Until we're sure this is a homicide and not an accidental death, I want everything we see and hear kept between us and the other law officers." He peered into Shandra's eyes. "Is that clear?"

She sighed. "Yes. You know I don't tell others what you discover in your investigations."

"I just want to make myself clear." He led Shandra to her Jeep. "See you at home." Ryan opened the driver's side door for her. "I'm going to run to the Huckleberry Police Station and call the victim's family. I'll be home in a couple of hours."

Shandra nodded. "I'm sorry you always have to call the families."

"It's not something I like to do, but as the investigating officer, it helps me to gather more information."

"Like her allergy." Shandra slid in behind the steering wheel. "See you later."

He closed the driver's door and backed up.

The vehicle started and Shandra drove down the street. His feet slowly carried him to his SUV. Calling the family was never easy but it did get him more insight into the victims.

~*~

"Yes, Emma was violently allergic to bees. Her allergist told us when she was a child to keep all raw honey away from her as it could contain bee venom, that's how allergic she is—was." Mrs. Wickes sniffed. After Ryan's initial introduction and then telling her

45

about her daughter, it had taken the women nearly five minutes to calm down. Mr. Wickes had taken over the phone at that point, asking more specific questions that Ryan had no answers for, yet.

"Do you know if your daughter carried an epinephrine autoinjector in her purse or on her person?" Ryan asked. He found it odd that a woman so allergic to bees would have only an injection in her toiletry bag and not with her.

"Yes. She carried one in her purse, and when she was out hiking or running, she carried one in a fanny pack." The woman's voice grew in strength. "Why, didn't she use her injection?"

"She didn't have a purse with her. She was on a massage table." Ryan wasn't going to be the one to tell this woman her daughter had been found naked.

"Massage table? How on earth did she get stung by a bee on a massage table?" the woman's voice became stronger. "What kind of place was she at?"

"Did she tell you where she was going?" Ryan asked, hoping to keep the woman from storming into the lodge.

"Last I knew she was in Las Vegas." There was a pause. "Wait a minute? You said you were a Weippe County Detective. Do you mean she was in Idaho? Emma was here in Idaho and didn't even contact us?" The woman started crying again.

"What's the matter with you?" the gruff voice of Mr. Wickes asked.

"I'm just asking questions about your daughter. I'm trying to learn all I can to help the forensic pathologists establish if your daughter's death was an accident." Ryan ran a hand over his face. He'd avoided saying anything about his thoughts so far.

"What do you mean if it was an accident? What else could it have been?" the man's voice lowered. Ryan assumed so his wife wouldn't hear him.

"I won't know until I get the results back from the state. I'll let you know what I find." Ryan hung up the phone on the desk in a small office at the Huckleberry Police Station. There were only two officers and a Police Chief in the small town. Most of the patrolling in the area was done by the county deputies.

He clicked on the monitor on the desk, accessed the FBI database and found Egan Trower still worked for the FBI. Ryan settled back in the desk chair. There were two people he could contact to learn more about Trower. He dived into his email and sent a chatty, how are you doing, have you heard I married and oh, what can you tell me about Egan Trower?

After sending the email to his friend in the bureau, Ryan turned off the computer and exited the office.

Hazel, the switchboard operator who seemed to volunteer twenty-four-seven, looked up from a cooking magazine. "Heard you caught a suspicious death at the lodge. That pretty new wife of yours going to help you solve it?"

Ryan groaned. "I don't know. She's a witness."

The woman slapped her magazine down on the desk and sat up straight. "Really? Then you know she's going to be belly-button deep in solving it."

"Yeah, that's what I'm afraid of."

Chapter Seven

Sheba stretched after rising from her spot in front of the dead fireplace and walked to the front door.

Shandra studied her large furry dog. "Is Ryan coming home?"

"Woof!" The dog's voice echoed through the great room.

"I guess that means you're going to take a look around." Shandra placed the laptop, she'd been using to research allergies to bees, on the coffee table and walked to the door. "Enjoy the brisk evening air," she said as the dog bounded out into the growing darkness.

That was one good thing about having a dog as big as a bear, there were few things that would try and fight her. However, the dog was a huge coward and would probably knock the door down getting in if something menacing out in the forest approached her.

Banging at the backdoor sent Shandra down the hall. She opened the door and her employee, Lil, stood with her arms full of chopped wood.

"There's a nip to the air tonight. Thought you might like to light a fire." She stomped down the hall to the great room and dumped the split lengths into the firewood box. A quick scan of the room and she asked, "Where's Ryan?"

Wondering if the woman was ill, Shandra stepped close to her and studied her face. Lil never asked about Ryan or had too many good things to say about him. They got off on the wrong foot back when Ryan had thought Lil killed her lover.

"Why are you interested in Ryan?" She reached out and touched the woman's forehead below a purple stocking cap.

Lil backed up, sputtering. "There's no need to take my temperature. I was just askin'." The woman spun on her heel and stomped back out the door she'd arrived through.

Shandra wandered into the kitchen and started water to boil in the tea kettle. Lil hadn't wanted her to know why she was looking for Ryan. Interesting…

Barking and the flash of light through the kitchen window meant Ryan had arrived. She pulled another cup out of the cupboard and plopped a tea bag in each cup.

The tea was steeped and waiting for him on the counter when Ryan finally came through the back door. It had been an unusually long amount of time for him to park his work vehicle under the lean-to off the barn and walk to the house.

"It smells like the holidays have arrived three months early," Ryan said, walking into the kitchen.

"I felt like tea with some comforting spices

tonight." Shandra sat on one of the stools at the counter. "You want to sit here or in the great room?"

Ryan kissed her cheek and picked up the mug waiting for him. "Great room."

She nodded, picked up her cup, and followed him. They sat on the couch, touching shoulders and sipping the hot liquid.

When she couldn't stand it any longer, she asked, "What did Lil want to talk to you about?"

"How do you know I talked to Lil?" He sipped his tea.

"She was in here earlier looking for you and you took a long time coming in after arriving." She shifted slightly, tucking a foot under her, and studying her husband.

He grinned. "Always putting two and two together aren't you." He put the cup on the coffee table and faced her. "Lil asked me to run a background check on some man who's moved to Huckleberry."

"Why would she want you to do that?" Shandra stared at Ryan. She could tell the reason was comical to him.

"Because he's been flirting with her at the donut shop and asked her out to dinner." He started laughing.

She didn't see anything funny about it. "Why would she want a background check?"

"Because she likes him and doesn't want to be swept off her feet by a serial killer." He raised his hands. "Her words."

Shandra burst out laughing.

"But you can't let her know I told you. I promised I wouldn't say a word to anyone." Ryan said, slowly sobering up.

"Can you do that? Do a background check for no reason?" Shandra asked, stifling her mirth.

"Not really. There is no legal reason for me to run one. I'll ask around about him and if I can find out where he came from give someone on a force there a call." He sighed. "I needed that bit of nonsense tonight."

Shandra put a hand on his arm. "Talking to the Wickes was that bad?"

"Yes, and no. It makes me think even more that she didn't accidently die from an allergy."

Shandra listened as Ryan told her about how the mother had said Emma always carried an injection to counteract her allergic reaction with her.

"But she was in a robe inside a building where there wasn't any chance of her coming in contact with a bee," Shandra said, hoping for Valerie's sake the allergic reaction was accidental.

"It's true there was no reason for her to need her epinephrine autoinjector. But there should have been one in her purse as well as her cosmetic bag." Ryan leaned back. "Her mother said she always had one with her."

"So where did the one from her purse go? If it was in her purse when she locked it in the locker, who could get in the locker and take it out? Were they afraid Emma might be able to get herself down the hall to the locker?" Shandra leaned forward and pulled a note pad toward her. She picked up a pen and wrote, *who has access to lockers*.

"We can't do anything more than speculate tonight. By noon tomorrow I should have the preliminary forensic evaluation." Ryan stood. "Let's get some sleep."

Shandra grabbed the two cups and carried them into the kitchen. Turning off the kitchen lights, she walked to the back door and whistled for Sheba. The big goof of a dog enjoyed her romps in the forest.

Within minutes the shaggy mutt arrived at the door. Her tongue hung out one side of her open mouth.

"What were you chasing?" Shandra asked, closing and locking the door as Sheba lumbered down the hall ahead of her.

In the bedroom, Sheba lay down on the crib size foam dog bed along one wall. Ryan was in the shower. Shandra changed into her pajamas and slipped into bed. Even though today wasn't the first time she'd found a body, the position Emma was in made her wonder if she'd walked in rather than stood in the hall if she could have helped the woman. For all she knew Emma had heard her voice and wanted to call out for help and couldn't because of the swelling from her allergy.

Shandra closed her eyes, listened to the steady stream of water from the shower, and willed her body to relax.

~*~

Grandmother sat on the top of a row of lockers that looked like the ones at the lodge. Shandra peered up at her. "What are you doing here, Ella?"

Every dream Shandra had with her grandmother, she never spoke. This dream was no different. The old woman raised a hand and pointed to a garden full of beautiful flowers. As Shandra stared at the colors, they came to life. The flowers danced around a tall evergreen tree as if in a ballet.

A vine appeared.

The flowers all stopped frolicking and ran, hiding behind a tree.

The vine continued to the tree, winding around until all that could be seen were its dark green boughs.

One by one the flowers appeared, but they didn't go near the tree.

"What do these flowers have to do with Emma's death?" Shandra asked. Flowers attracted bees, but she didn't understand what that had to do with who killed Emma.

~*~

Ryan headed to work at his usual time. Shandra finished up the dishes from breakfast and walked out to the barn. It was the end of summer with cooler weather and the inevitable winter snow that would keep her from the mountain and the clay deposit on her property. Today was the perfect day to collect a few buckets to give her enough clay to use through the winter months.

She grabbed two halters and headed to the corral. Apple and Sammy, her mare and packhorse, would be ready for a ride up the mountain. Shandra and Ryan had gone on a ride the previous week, but she'd been busy putting the final touches on a vase and hadn't had time to go since. She'd finished that piece yesterday before heading down the mountain for a massage.

"Where you goin'?" Lil asked, stepping out of the barn with Lewis, her cat, wrapped around her neck like an orange fur stole.

"Figured I'd go up and dig some clay. I want to get several batches purified before the cold weather hits and I can't dig anymore." She caught Apple and walked over to Sammy, slipping the halter on him.

"Care if me and Sunshine come along?" Lil asked,

wistfully.

"I don't mind at all." Shandra smiled. Her employee said exactly what she felt and didn't hide her feelings about people and what she thought. To have her ask to come along had Shandra wondering if she planned to say anything about the man she'd asked Ryan to check out.

Lil caught her old palomino mare.

All three horses were saddled and ready to go in fifteen minutes. Shandra put two spades on the packsaddle along with four five-gallon buckets.

They headed up the mountain following the now well-worn trail. Shandra had been taking this path every couple of months from May to October to dig the clay that made her pottery. The pocket of clay she found before purchasing the property was a good two miles up hill from the buildings.

The horses meandered up the mountainside, knowing the destination. Shandra settled back in her saddle, enjoying the sights of leaves on the bushes and leafy trees starting to turn as they rode higher and the air became brisker.

"Won't be long and these leaves will be as purty as the wildflowers were last spring," Lil mused.

Shandra twisted in her saddle, studying the woman riding behind the packhorse. She'd never made a statement like that out loud before. She smiled and replied, "Yes, they will."

She peered forward happy to see Lil in such a good mood. It did appear the older woman was feeling something for the man who'd caught her attention enough she wanted Ryan to check him out.

At the clay pocket, they dismounted and both

grasped a spade and began filling the buckets.

"Seems to me, the clay is getting a richer color to it," Lil said.

"It is. The deeper I dig into this pocket the purer and more colorful the clay becomes. I hope it holds out until I no longer want to make pottery. I enjoy using the gifts of the earth that I dig up to make my vases." Shandra stood with the shovel sunk in the clay and stared up at the blue sky with a wisp of white cloud floating by. "I never want to leave this place." She glanced over at Lil. "It had to have been hard for your grandparents to leave here. And I understand why you wouldn't." Lil had come with the property like a stray cat. She'd refused to leave when it was sold to pay for her grandparents stay in a nursing home. The new owners ended up having her put in jail for trespassing. When Shandra met the woman, she didn't see why they couldn't get along and that was how Lil became her righthand woman.

The older woman nodded. "This is the closest thing to heaven a person can find. Don't see any reason to leave it."

They both lifted a bucket up, and Shandra used one hand to buckle the strap around the handle to hold it on the pack saddle. When all four buckets were secured and the spades tied onto the pack, they headed back down the mountain. Shandra's mind wandered to yesterday and if Ryan had discovered anything else about the woman's death.

Chapter Eight

The words on the monitor popped out at Ryan. *Egan Trower had asked for 90 days leave. Before he took leave, he'd been handling a woman who was going to give evidence against a money laundering organization. The woman changed her mind and ducked out on him and the investigation.*

Ryan replied to the email. *Was Emma Wickes the witness?*

He waited, rereading the information his friend in the bureau had sent him about Trower. It seemed Emma had ditched him. But why had the man taken leave to follow her here, to Huckleberry Lodge? Had he tried to prey on Emma's fear and make her think the money laundering gang was after her? He'd witnessed Trower do some sneaky stuff back in Chicago when Ryan was undercover in a gang. But they all lost informants. Why had he followed Ms. Wickes?

Can't confirm or deny. But he and the witness had

become VERY close. Came the reply.

Ryan tapped a finger on the desk top. Had the informant been Emma Wickes? When she dropped Trower to go back to Tabor Maxmillan had the FBI agent gone after her? But she hadn't run to Maxmillan. She'd gone to Huckleberry Lodge. Was she trying to figure out her feelings for the two men? All the questions weren't getting answered by tossing them around in his head.

He'd also received the lengthy file on the money laundering boss in Las Vegas. Ryan had skimmed the pages of the document and now realized he needed to know everything he could about Maxmillan. Either he or Trower had possible reasons to want to harm or kill the victim.

Reading through the documents, a picture caught his attention. It was a surveillance photo of the boss and a pretty brunette who looked a lot like the victim. Ryan enlarged the photo and stared at it. He'd thought the woman had been working for Maxmillan. It looked like she'd been sleeping with him. The comments from the agent who took the photo mentioned Maxmillan and his girlfriend.

He scrolled back through the documents. There it was. The money laundering boss was married. Ryan leaned back in his chair. "Had this Maxmillan been the married man the victim told Valerie about?" He studied the photo of the two. She was definitely staring at him like a woman in love. This added another component to the murder. Did the wife know about Emma and her husband?

Ryan pulled up the file with the notes Speaks had taken from people who had been in the spa area at the time of the murder. Trower was the only name he recognized. The file on Maxmillan had a list of the members of his organization. He printed that out and decided to compare this with the guests staying at the lodge.

~*~

After spreading the clay out on boards to dry, Shandra went in the house to clean up. She'd decided to head to Ruthie's Diner for lunch. Her friend served the best burgers in town and usually knew all the gossip. She'd not only see what the grapevine in Huckleberry had to say about the death at the lodge but maybe, someone might know who the man was that had Lil smitten.

As she pulled out of her driveway and onto the county road, Shandra texted Ryan, she'd be at Ruthie's in forty-five minutes if he wanted to meet for lunch.

Her phone buzzed, and she pulled over in a driveway to look at the message.

At the lodge. Can meet you at Ruthie's at 1.

I can come to the lodge, she responded.

No. I'll meet you at Ruthie's.

She smiled. He was trying to keep her out of the investigation. *Ok.*

Pulling back onto the road, she headed to town. Ryan had listened to her retelling of the dream she'd had. He couldn't make any sense of it either. He'd believed in her dreams before she'd realized her grandmother and the dreams weren't her subconscious making up for all the time she'd missed with her paternal grandmother. Now when she had a dream with her grandmother in them, she always told him, and they worked together to figure out what the dream meant.

She entered Huckleberry from the east on County Road 15. A right on Main Street and she drove by the Daily Donut. She glanced in the windows wondering if Lil would meet her admirer here today. It was one of the places her employee frequented the most.

A right on Huckleberry Street and Shandra drove by Dimensions Gallery owned by her friends Ted and Naomi Norton. She glanced in the front window to see which of her vases the couple was featuring this week. Naomi had reached out to her when she moved to Huckleberry ten years ago, and they'd become her first friends in the area.

Parking in front of Ruthie's Diner, she grinned. A fire a year ago had ruined the interior, but the changes Ruthie, Treat, and Ruthie's uncle had made to the place attracted even more of the tourist traffic. It looked like a diner out of the 50s with jukeboxes on the tables, black LPs, and posters of 50s musical entertainers hung on the walls. They'd even put in black and white checkerboard tile flooring.

Treat had found jukeboxes, that while looking real, were enhanced with modern technology. They all synced so when one table played a song, it came out of speakers at all the booths. She walked into the diner to the crooning of "Blue Moon" by Mel Tormé.

While she preferred jazz and lately drumming and flute music, the smooth tone and melodic words grabbed her.

Ruthie walked out of the kitchen with three burger baskets and nodded for her to sit at an open table by the counter.

Shandra took a seat and scanned the diner. It was busy for being the tail end of the lunch hour. She noticed several locals shoving empty baskets to the center of the table and heading to the cash register at the counter.

Ruthie came over as her waitress took the customers' money at the counter. "Are you eating alone or is Ryan joining you?"

"Ryan is coming. But I'd love to get a caramel milkshake now. I worked up an appetite digging clay this morning." Shandra knew the menu by heart.

"I can get that going for you."

Ruthie turned to leave and Shandra asked, "Any chance you can join me until Ryan gets here?"

Her friend grinned. "I am the boss. And now that Uncle Orin is cooking, I can take all the breaks I want. I'll grab that shake and be right back."

Shandra took off her jacket and settled into the seat.

Ruthie returned with the shake and a soda for herself. She slid into the chair across from Shandra as she placed the drinks on the table. "What have you been up to?" Her friend's brown face glowed with happiness.

"Marriage is good for you," Shandra said, thinking Ruthie glowed even more than usual.

Her friend's dark brown eyes sparkled as she leaned over the table toward Shandra. "We haven't told anyone, so keep this quiet." She placed a hand on her belly. "We're having a baby in six months."

Shandra kept her voice down. "Congratulations! I didn't know you were ready to start having kids."

"We've been trying since we married." Ruthie narrowed her eyes. "You and I are not getting younger. If you wait much longer, you'll be considered a high-risk pregnancy."

Shandra heard this from her in-laws every day. She and Ryan were enjoying being just the two of them. While they both enjoyed his nieces and nephews, they weren't ready to take the plunge of parenthood. Shandra because of the turmoil in her life being raised by two people who didn't really want or love her. She knew she would never do that to a child, having lived that way. With Ryan's dangerous job, she didn't want to end up raising a child alone and would never remarry and subject a child to a stepfather.

"We're thinking about it," she replied as her friend kept watching her.

"You can't let your past keep you from leaving your mark on the future." Ruthie sipped her drink. "I know Maxwell is having a hard time keeping this a secret. But I want to get past the first trimester before we tell anyone. My doctor—"

"Are you going to Alex?" Shandra interrupted.

"No." Ruthie's cheeks grew darker. "I didn't want to go through the pregnancy with him, knowing how badly Miranda and Alex are trying for a baby. I'm going to a doctor in Warner."

"That's considerate," Shandra said, wondering how her friend Miranda would take the news.

Ruthie shrugged. "Why did you want to talk to me?"

"What have you heard about the death at the lodge?" Shandra sipped her shake and watched her friend.

"That you and Valerie found the body." She tipped her head. "I guess with as many bodies as you find, it might not be a good idea to have to worry about a child."

"Anything else? Rumors?" Shandra ignored the comment.

"The woman has family around here but no one knew she was here." Ruthie took a sip of her drink and said, "In fact, they say it was Valerie's cousin and the two of them never got along."

"Really?" Shandra didn't think Valerie had killed her cousin, but if there had been bad blood between them the police would dig it up. "Why didn't they get along?"

"You know, the cousin was pretty, Valerie was, well Valerie." Ruthie glanced at the door as it jingled. "Your date is here." She stood, taking her glass with her.

"Ruthie, you look pretty today," Ryan said, sliding into the chair, she'd just vacated.

"Thank you. What can I get you?"

"An iced tea, cheeseburger, and fries." He glanced over at Shandra. "I see you've started."

"Only on this. I'll have my usual," she told Ruthie.

"I'll have that for you in a few." Her friend walked to the kitchen.

"You didn't mind me saying Ruthie looked pretty, did you?" Ryan asked. His gaze was locked on her.

Shandra smiled. "No. She is beaming." Nodding toward the kitchen, she said, "And she has a good reason why."

Chapter Nine

His phone buzzed as Ryan stood at the counter to pay for their lunch. He handed the money and check to Shandra and walked out of the diner.

"Greer."

"Detective Greer, this is Sheila Rickman at the State Forensic lab. I have your preliminary results as to cause of death. I'll know more when blood work and other samples are tested."

"Was it from a bee sting?" he asked.

"I couldn't find a spot anywhere on her body for a bee to have stung her, but she did die from anaphylactic shock brought on by a hypersensitive allergic reaction. Once I have her stomach contents analyzed I can see if there are any of the normal allergens. But bee venom and honey would be hard to find in stomach contents."

"Did you notice if there had been a struggle of any kind?" Knowing the victim was deathly allergic to bees, he didn't think someone would be able to slip her honey or get her near a bee without a fight.

"I didn't see anything that would suggest there had been any kind of struggle. Everything I can discern says she laid down on the massage table and her allergic reaction hit her hard and quickly. I doubt she would have even had the ability to get off the table once the anaphylaxis started."

That explained why she hadn't called out. But why did someone take her epinephrine from her purse? "Thanks. As soon as you learn more, don't hesitate to call."

He ended the conversation as Shandra walked out of the diner. "Are you headed home?"

"Have you had a chance to check out Lil's friend?" she asked.

Ryan grinned and shook his head. "No. I've been tied up with the suspicious death investigation all morning. Why?"

"I thought I'd pop in at the Daily Donut and see if Mark knows who the man is." Her eyes twinkled as she walked to her Jeep and slid behind the wheel.

He had no doubt his wife would find out more about the man by quizzing locals than he could by putting the name through any database.

Even though he'd spent the morning at the lodge, he headed back. He'd gone over the two rooms closely for anything that resembled honey or parts of bees. Nothing had cropped up. He wanted to talk to the spa manager. There had to be an explanation for what had caused the woman's death. And he wanted to have a word with Trower.

Alice Dremple was in her fifties with orange hair.

Not the fading red of a redhead trying to keep their color, this woman had full-on orange hair like someone going to a costume party. Her round face and large teeth had Ryan thinking of a Jack-o-lantern.

"Ms. Dremple—"

"Alice. Call me Alice, I don't care to be reminded of the scum I married." She narrowed her eyes and crossed her arms under her ample breasts, resting them on her round mid-section.

"Alice. Is there a protocol Valerie should have followed to bring a guest into the spa?" He'd wondered why Valerie had secreted her cousin into the spa when she kept saying they'd not talked in years.

"We ask that all guests of the people working here go through the registration desk. If an employee wants to give a family member a procedure, the person must fill out the health screening form, otherwise the spa is liable for any mishaps that may occur." She made a face. "I want it on the record, we knew nothing about her cousin being in the spa. We are not liable for someone who didn't follow the rules."

Ryan wrote that down in his notepad. "I see. And where were you yesterday afternoon?"

"I was in the office with the bookkeeper running through the list of supplies that needed ordered." She uncrossed her arms and slammed a fist into her palm. "If I had seen the woman in the breakroom or anywhere else, I would have made her go through the proper paperwork. As for Valerie…I'm discussing what to do about her with Meredith today."

"Is it customary for someone to hang around in the spa area waiting to see if an appointment isn't filled and taking that time?" He found it odd that Trower was doing that in hopes of getting a massage, especially since the deceased had been a spur of the moment spa client.

"Usually, no. Very few people want to hang around in the spa for hours waiting on the off chance someone will cancel. Why do you ask?" Alice had her arms crossed again.

"That was what one of the people we interviewed said he was doing yesterday afternoon. I thought it odd, but I don't go to spas."

Alice looked him up and down. "You should join your wife for a couple's massage sometime."

"I'll think about it." The words sounded sincere but his head wasn't going for it. The only couple's massage he planned to do was him massaging Shandra or vice-versa. No one else in the room.

"Can you tell me where you keep the honey that is set out for your clients?" While the autopsy report couldn't concretely state that foul play had killed the victim or that it had been homicide rather than an accident, Ryan had a gut feeling it had been well thought out, which is what circled him back to Valerie. It was hard to imagine the cousin coming to the spa and someone just happened to be there that knew about her allergy. And conveniently there was raw honey.

"Yes. It's in the closet in the breakroom. I don't order large amounts at a time because it hardens faster than pasteurized honey you get at the grocery store." Alice set off toward the women's side of the spa. She stopped and pointed for him to go through the men's side.

As they'd talked in a corner of the registration area, he'd noticed the man and young woman who'd manned the desk the day before had been listening intently to the conversation.

Ryan went through the men's side and came out the same as the day before. Alice stood in the hallway waiting for him. He followed the woman down the hall. The one room without police tape was being used.

"Who is giving a massage this afternoon?" he asked.

"Not Valerie. She's on leave until we figure out what to do," snapped Alice.

"Were all your rooms booked today?" he asked, having noticed people sitting in the lounge.

At the breakroom, Alice faced him. "You're keeping us out of the massage rooms has backed things up. We had to call and cancel several of the later appointments. One room and two people booked to have massages is cutting into the profit."

"Who is giving massages today?" he asked again.

"Laurie Gordon. She was here yesterday. And Louise. Yesterday was her day off." Alice walked across the room and stood on her toes to open a cupboard high on the wall. Six jars of honey were lined up in a row.

"Are any jars missing?" Ryan asked, pulling out his phone and taking a picture.

"No, there were six jars here the last time I checked."

"Whereabouts on the premises are the other jars?" He noticed one on the table in the breakroom and snapped a quick photo.

"This one, and one in the registration area on the tea tray."

"None in the lounge?" he asked.

"No. We only have cool liquids there." Alice led him back down the hall to the lounge. A man and two women were wrapped in the white robes, lounging on what appeared to be soft leather chairs.

Alice smiled at the people and walked over to a chrome and mirror beverage cart. A clear water dispenser had leaves, cucumber slices, and lemon slices floating along with ice cubes. Next to the water dispenser was a plate of fancy cookies and a small bowl of unsalted mixed nuts.

Ryan took a photo of the serving cart.

"Why are you so interested in our honey? Does it have anything to do with that woman's death?" Alice asked in a whisper.

"Could be nothing." Ryan slipped his notepad into his pocket and headed out of the spa calling Sheriff Oldham to get a deputy to check the wastebaskets and dumpsters for an epinephrine pen and cell phone. Someone had to have disposed of those two items after making sure Ms. Wickes had been exposed to bee venom.

Chapter Ten

Brewing coffee and the sweet, yeasty aroma of donuts wafted around Shandra as she entered the Daily Donut. The business would only be open for another hour, but it smelled as good now as it did at 5 a.m. when they opened.

"Shandra, need some rolls for dinner? And I have a couple of Lil's favorite pastries left," Mark Surlee, the owner, said.

"If you have a loaf of the nine seed bread, I'll take that and the pastries for Lil." She stepped up to the counter. "I'm surprised you still have her favorites left this time of day."

Mark grinned. "I've been making more of them. Lil has been stopping in a lot lately."

This was why she came to the donut shop. "Really? And why does she come by here more?"

The man shook his head. "It's the darnedest thing. She and a new customer both sat down at a table at the same time about a month ago. You know Lil, she glared at him and said it was her table. He smiled at her and said, he'd be honored to share the table with such a pretty thing." Mark laughed. "I've never seen Lil blush, but she did, and then allowed him to sit at the table with her. They've been meeting up here several times a week since then. They sit over in the corner there and talk and laugh." He shook his head. "If you'd have told me Lil knew how to laugh, I would have said you were lying, but she's a changed person since meeting Harvey."

"Harvey what? Do you know where he came from and what he's doing here?" Shandra asked, taking the bread and pastries Mark had bagged while talking.

"Harvey Beatty. From talking to him, he's a retired professor. Not sure of what. His daughter lives in Warner, but he didn't want to live in the same town as her. It seems he doesn't get along with the son-in-law, but he wanted to be close enough to attend grandkids' functions."

Everything Mark had to say about Lil's crush sounded good to Shandra. "You'll let me know if he seems to be anything other than what he says?"

Mark nodded. "We all might find Lil a bit hard and too truthful, but we look out for our own. I've been keeping an eye on them."

"Thanks Mark." Shandra handed him more than the baked goods were worth and walked out of the shop. This was why she wanted to live in a small community. They looked out for one another.

~*~

After having the registration desk call up to Trower's room to see if he was in and discovering he wasn't, Ryan decided to check out the restaurant and bar. He found the man he wanted to talk to seated at the bar. A young couple sat at a table. The couple and the bartender were the only other people besides Trower.

Ryan took a stool beside the FBI Agent and ordered an iced tea.

Trower looked over. "Either you're an alcoholic or you're a cop."

"The second. Mr. Trower, can you tell me why you followed Ms. Wickes to Huckleberry Lodge?"

"Because I'm an idiot." He took a swallow of his drink.

"I've discovered you were one of the agents in charge of guarding Ms. Wickes while she waited to give evidence against a Tabor Maxmillan. What happened?"

The man looked at him with red-rimmed eyes. He'd either been up all night or had been sitting at the bar since it opened. "She was too sweet, too naïve, to have fallen for the likes of Maxmillan. Even after I showed her all the proof of his infidelity with women before her, she made up excuses for him." The man swallowed more of the amber liquid in his glass.

"Why were you showing her all of this when she had already agreed to testify against him?" Ryan had a feeling he knew what was coming.

"Because she still loved the creep. She was only testifying to get him to divorce his wife. She thought if she showed him she was willing to go that far to get him, he'd see how much she loved him."

Now Ryan was confused. "So did Maxmillan plan to divorce his wife to keep Ms. Wickes from testifying?" He couldn't think of any other reason for the victim to have left.

"Somehow he got word to her that he would do what she wanted. I think she left to get proof he was really going to get the divorce. But then she came here." He shook his head. "I think it was a ploy to get her out of our custody and then kill her." Trower studied him. "What was the cause of death?"

"Anaphylaxis."

The agent stared at him. "An allergic reaction?" He shook his head. "That doesn't make sense. She always carried her pen with her."

"You knew about her allergy?"

"Yeah, it was so severe it was in the file we were given on her." Trower's eyes watered. "It had to have been intentional."

"Who did you see in the spa area?" Ryan pulled out his notepad.

Trower stared at him. "I gave my information to the deputy yesterday."

"That was before I knew who you were. Come on, as one law enforcement officer to another, why did you hang out in the spa area? Did you see the woman enter the spa?"

The man swiveled the bar stool and sat facing him. "I was waiting in the coffee bar for Emma. She'd texted me and said she wanted to talk."

"How did she know you were here?" Ryan glanced up from the pad he was writing on.

The man's ears grew red. "I contacted her as soon as I'd learned she'd come here. Asked if I could talk with her. Not about testifying. About…us."

"You fell in love with the person you were guarding?" Ryan had heard of this happening.

The man's chin dipped to his chest. "I've never

believed in love at first sight, but when I walked through the door to take over the next shift, I felt as if I'd been punched in the gut. We talked while I was on duty. She was a sweet woman who got mixed up with the wrong person."

"Ok, back to my questions. What did you talk about, here, in the coffee bar?"

"Nothing. I saw her, she walked up to order, and a woman hurried up to her and they started talking. Next thing I know they are headed out of the coffee bar. I followed. I knew the woman who'd taken her away worked in the lodge because of her shirt, but when she took Emma through a door and I found it locked, I began to panic. I asked where the door went and discovered it was an employee entrance to the spa." He swiveled back to the bar and swallowed more of his drink. "I went in through the reception area and began searching for her."

His head twisted, he peered at Ryan cockeyed. "You might want to ask Bailey and Lance what they were doing in the spa area then."

"Bailey as in Bailey Ullrich, Emma's friend?" Ryan knew it was not a real friendship but he wanted to see what Trower said.

"Bailey Ullrich, as in body guard for Tabor Maxmillan."

"He knew where Ms. Wickes had run to?" This added to his assumption she'd been killed to keep her quiet about Maxmillan's business.

"Bailey went everywhere Emma went before she came to us. I'm assuming she was watching and waiting for a chance to get to Emma when she left thinking Maxmillan had crumpled."

"But if that's true, why didn't Ms. Ullrich take Emma somewhere and bury her? Why make it so public?" No, it didn't make sense that the bodyguard killed the woman. She was working for Maxmillan and it appeared the man wanted the victim alive. Had he really cared for her? Enough that he would have left the wife he hadn't left for all the other women?

"Who is this Lance you mentioned?"

"Lance Springer, Marcia Maxmillan's private investigator. She wanted Emma out of the picture and hired Lance to do it." Trower sneered. "It seems Emma won over most men's hearts."

"When and where did you see Springer?" Ryan had a feeling there were more suspects than he'd first imagined and that this would soon be a homicide and not an accidental death.

Chapter Eleven

Before leaving Huckleberry, Shandra decided to run by Valerie's and see if she could be of any help. The woman depended on her job at the lodge.

Valerie opened the door. She wore baggy sweats and a t-shirt.

"Is Josie at school?" Shandra asked, holding up Lil's pastries. She'd decided Valerie was a good cause to not take Lil's favorite pastry home.

"Yes, thank goodness. That way she doesn't know I'm out of a job." Valerie led the way into a small kitchen. She grabbed a mug out of the cupboard and poured coffee into it before topping off a mug that sat on the counter.

Shandra took a seat at the kitchen table and pulled out the two cherry filled turnovers. "I wanted to see how you were doing."

Tears pooled in Valerie's eyes. "Aunt Betty called my mom, and she called me, asking why I hadn't told

Betty Emma was here. I tried to tell her I didn't know until an hour before she was…gone."

"This has to be hard on you. Not only finding the body but it being family." A prickling on the back of Shandra's neck caused her to inhale slightly. What had that been?

"It's almost like they are blaming me for her death. All I did was invite her to get a massage to ease the tension I could see hunching her shoulders." Valerie took a big bite of the pastry and chewed.

Shandra didn't know what to say. She hadn't had time to learn what Ryan had discovered today. "Did it look like Emma was alone when she… where did you say you saw her?"

Valerie swallowed and took a sip of coffee before she said, "I saw her walk into the coffee bar, you know to the left of the lobby."

Shandra knew the coffee bar. Bailey had said Emma went down for a coffee. "Was she alone?"

Valerie stared at her. "She stood at the counter ordering all by herself. I don't think there was anyone meeting her." She lifted the pastry to her mouth. "But I was only focused on her, because I couldn't believe she'd come back." She took a bite.

"What do you mean, you couldn't believe she'd come back?" Shandra knew about how some families had feuds and grudges that kept them apart.

"She and her mom, my Aunt Betty, had a huge blowout when Emma left for Vegas. Emma wanted to be a dancer. Aunty Betty said all she would become was a hooker." Valerie raised an eyebrow. "From what I learned through one of Valerie's friends, she wasn't a hooker but darn close. She said Emma was a mistress to a rich man."

"Why do you think Emma came back?" Shandra picked up the coffee and sipped.

"From what she'd said, I'd guessed she was in trouble." Valerie played with the crumbling crust on the pastry. "You know, like the man who didn't want her knocked her up."

This was news she wondered if Ryan knew about. Surely the autopsy would have revealed how far along Emma was. "Are you sure? There hasn't been any mention of her being pregnant."

"She didn't actually come right out and say the man she was running from was the father of her baby. She did tell me she was pregnant and worried her mom would think she had been walking the streets in Vegas." Valerie took another big bite and chewed.

Shandra chewed on the information and sipped coffee. Could this be why she'd changed her mind to testify against the man Maxmillan? He was the father, and she didn't want to be the one to put him in jail. Did he know she was carrying his child? Was that why she'd been killed?

So many questions.

The phone on the kitchen wall rang. Valerie chewed quickly and swallowed the bite down with coffee before answering the phone.

"Hello?" She listened and nodded.

"I am sorry. I only wanted to treat my cousin." She nodded some more.

"Thank you! I appreciate that." Valerie hung up the phone and turned to Shandra. A smile lit her face. "That was Meredith. She said she'd talked with Alice and I was to come back to work tomorrow. That while I had not followed the rules, they were booked up and needed me to work. But I had to promise to abide by all the rules and give up my key to the employee door." She drew in a long breath and let it out like a yoga student.

"That's good news." Shandra put down her coffee and stood. "I need to get going. I only told Lil I'd be gone for lunch and now it's almost dinner time."

"Josie will be home soon." Valerie stood. "Don't forget your pastry."

"Let Josie have it when she gets home." Shandra bid good-bye and headed out to her Jeep. Before she pulled onto the street, she texted Ryan. *Did the autopsy say Emma was pregnant*?

~*~

By the time Ryan left the bar, he'd filled up two pages on his notepad. And now he was headed to the lodge offices to ask Meredith for the room number of Lance Springer.

His phone vibrated in his pocket. He pulled it out. A text from Shandra. The sentence stopped his forward motion. Pregnant?

Ryan immediately dialed Sheila Rickman at the State Forensic Lab.

"Sheila," she answered.

"This is Detective Greer. Have you started the autopsy on my anaphylactic victim from yesterday?"

"I was just working on her."

"I have reason to believe she may have been pregnant. Is there a way you can tell and we can do a paternity check?" He wondered if the baby belonged to Maxmillan or someone else.

"I can have the urine tested for HCG and I can vacuum the uterus and see how far along she was, if there is a pregnancy."

"Thanks. It could be important to why she died." Ryan disconnected and continued down the hall to the lodge offices.

The lodge offices had one main secretary. He stepped in the small office and held out his badge. "Is Ms. Gamble in?"

"She is. I'll give her a call." The secretary held a short conversation and returned the phone to the base. "She'll be out in a minute." The woman motioned to a chair by the door.

Ryan backed up and sat. He scribbled the text from Shandra in his notebook and wondered if Trower was the father and had the victim been trying to pass the baby off as Maxmillan's?

The whisper of pant legs brushing and muffled steps growing closer made him glance down the hall.

Ms. Gamble strode his way. "Detective, what can I help you with today?"

Ryan stood. "I'd like to know the room number of Lance Springer and to see a readout of all your current guests."

She studied him for several seconds before asking her secretary to print out what he requested. "Why do you need a list of our guests?" she asked.

"Because more and more people keep popping up who knew the dead woman."

Her mouth dropped open and snapped closed so fast he almost believed he hadn't seen the shock on the woman's face.

"I thought the death was accidental? Alice said you were asking about the raw honey. I'd assumed the woman died of an allergic reaction." She took the papers the secretary held out to her and headed down the hallway to her office.

Ryan followed. He waited until they were in her office before he responded. "We have reason to believe it was not an accident." He reached across the desk and picked up the sheets of paper.

"You mean she was…murdered?" Ms. Gamble's eyes widened.

"There is reason to believe she has been a victim of homicide." Ryan scanned the list of people staying at the lodge. His gaze came to a halt on Mr. and Mrs. Tabor Maxmillan. What were they doing here?

He glanced at the date beside their names. The day before yesterday. "What is this date? Is it when they arrived?" He pointed to the date beside the name of someone else. He didn't want the woman to inadvertently tell the Maxmillan's he was interested in them.

"Yes, that's the date that gentleman arrived." Her gaze drifted over the name.

Ryan returned to studying the list. Trower arrived the day after Ms. Wickes and Ms. Ullrich. Springer arrived the next day and the day after that the Maxmillans arrived.

"Thank you. This is all very helpful." Ryan stood. "We've collected all the evidence from the two rooms. You may use them again."

"Thank you. Our spa services were getting backed up." Ms. Gamble picked up the phone.

Ryan left the office in search of Springer. It was too much of a coincidence that all the people who had the most to lose because of Ms. Wickes testimony and baby were at the Huckleberry Lodge during her death.

Chapter Twelve

Halfway home, Shandra received a text from Ryan. *Dinner at the Lodge tonight?*

It appeared he'd be working late and at the lodge. She replied, *Yes*, and immediately called Lil.

"That's some lunch you're takin'," the woman said in her usual brusque fashion.

Shandra laughed. If the woman hadn't of answered gruffly, she would have thought something was wrong. "Lunch has been over for some time. I was on my way home and Ryan asked me to have dinner at the lodge with him. Do you mind taking care of Sheba's dinner tonight?"

"She's no trouble. Lewis likes when Sheba hangs out with us." The older woman's tone said, she also enjoyed Sheba's company. It couldn't be for protection; the big goofy dog was scared of her own shadow.

"Thank you. I'm not sure what time I'll get home."

"I'll turn on the outside lights when it gets dark."

Shandra had no idea what she would do without the woman if she decided to move somewhere else. "Thank you!"

"No problem, gotta check on the horses anyway," Lil said gruffly and ended the conversation.

The woman didn't like to show any softness, which made Shandra wonder about the man who Mark said made Lil laugh. The only time Lil laughed was watching Lewis or Sheba's antics.

She made a U-turn at one of the neighbor's driveways and headed back to Huckleberry and the lodge. Knowing about the riff between Emma and her mother and the fact the woman had come home when she was pregnant, had Shandra wondering if the pregnancy had scared Emma more than knowing the head of a money laundering gang was after her?

Driving through Huckleberry, she noticed the Dimensions Gallery lights still on. A quick check of the dash clock said it was ten after five. This time of year, the lull between summer tourists and wintertime skiers, the gallery closed at five unless someone asked to come by at a later time. Ted and Naomi lived above the gallery, making it easy for them to accommodate anyone who wished to come in at odd hours.

She parked in front of the building and stared through the large plate glass windows. Ted was showing an older man in a wheelchair around the gallery. It was apparent the man must have arrived just as they were closing. She turned the Jeep back out into the street and continued out the other side of town and up the road to the lodge.

Sitting in the parking lot, she texted Ryan for his location.

Restaurant.

Inside, she discovered Ryan sitting at a table in the far corner. He'd stood when she walked in the door to catch her attention and sat back down.

She had to travel a round-about course to get to the table. It appeared a wealthy looking couple had been a magnet to the serving staff. Business must have been slow lately for so many of the waiters and waitresses to be falling over themselves to help the couple.

"Who are they?" she asked, taking a seat beside Ryan on the bench seat facing the room.

"Mr. and Mrs. Tabor Maxmillan."

She studied him to make sure he wasn't kidding. "Maxmillan, as in the man Emma wanted to leave his wife?"

"The same." He held up his nearly empty glass of iced tea and a waitress broke away from the gathering.

"What would you like?" the young woman asked Shandra.

"I'll have iced tea. Who are those people?" she asked, to see what the woman had to say.

"They're the Maxmillan's. They own several casinos in Las Vegas and Mr. Maxmillan said he is always looking for good wait staff." The woman glanced over her shoulder. "It would be fun to work in Vegas, but I don't think I'd want to work for the wife." The waitress shuddered. "She's been giving orders right and left." The waitress took Ryan's glass and went to the kitchen.

"Do you think they came here looking to add staff to one of their casinos?" Shandra asked,

"No, it's a poor excuse to cover for the fact they were here when a person they knew died." Ryan continued to stare at them.

The man casually turned his head and stared back.

Ryan didn't break his gaze.

Shandra studied the man. He had a pretty face for a man. Which made it hard to believe he was mixed up in illegal activities. That was probably why Emma fell for him and didn't believe he could be the head of a money laundering syndicate.

Tabor Maxmillan nonchalantly returned his attention to the woman beside him.

"He's pretty calm for someone who lost a mistress and possibly a baby," Shandra said.

"I haven't talked to them yet. After my conversation with Lance Springer I wanted to fortify myself before contacting them."

"Who is Lance Springer?" Shandra smiled at the waitress as she returned with their drinks.

"Are you ready to order?"

They both ordered steak and baked potato with a salad.

"Lance Springer is Mrs. Maxmillan's private investigator."

Shandra studied the back of the woman next to Mr. Maxmillan. "Why does she have a private investigator? To keep tabs on her husband?"

"According to Springer, he is paid a hefty monthly fee to, as you say, keep tabs on the woman's husband and to pay off the women Maxmillan trifles with."

She twisted on the bench seat and peered into Ryan's face. "Emma wasn't willing to be bought off, was she?"

He shook his head. "Springer said she was the only woman in Tabor's life who refused a hundred thousand dollars to leave the man alone."

"Does he, this investigator, know she may have been pregnant? If so, that could have put her in danger from Mrs. Maxmillan." Shandra wondered how much the investigator had dug up on Emma. Did he know about her allergy?

Before she could ask, Ryan said, "I didn't bring up the pregnancy, but I did mention the allergy. He knew about that. He'd followed her when she picked up a new pen at the pharmacy and casually asked her what a pretty thing like her would need something like that for." Ryan let out a large huff of breath. "She told him because she was deathly allergic to bee stings." He shook his head. "An innocent comment to the wrong person, in this case her lover's wife's investigator, could have caused her death."

Shandra stared at the back of the woman again. "Do you know anything about her? Mrs. Maxmillan?"

"Cathleen is digging up information for me."

"Good." Ryan's older sister worked dispatch for the Weippe County Sheriff's Department. On several of the murder investigations, Shandra's dreams had helped solve, Cathleen's help in getting information had pulled the dreams and the evidence together.

Ryan nodded as the waitress brought their dinner. He'd watched the Maxmillan's enter the restaurant shortly after he'd sat down. They had yet to order a meal. At the rate they were going about dinner, he'd have to eat slow and order dessert and coffee before they would head to the penthouse suite they had procured for a week.

He wasn't sure if Springer had called Marcia Maxmillan as soon as Ryan had left the investigator's hotel room. If so, as soon as he mentioned his name, she'd know he'd been poking around in her business.

No sense ruining his dinner. Ryan cut into his steak and focused his attention on the food and Shandra until the waitress came to take their plates away.

Glancing at the other table, the Maxmillan's had finally been served their meal. Ryan picked up the dessert menu. "What would you like for dessert?"

"Wow! You're going all out tonight," Shandra teased. "I'll have the caramel apple pie, please."

"Sounds good. Make it two, I know she won't share with me."

The waitress smiled and headed to the kitchen with their dirty plates and dessert order.

Springer walked into the restaurant. He scanned the room, his gaze lingered on Ryan, before he walked over to the Maxmillan table.

"Who is that?" Shandra picked up her drink.

"The investigator."

"The husband must know about the investigator for him to walk up to the table like an old friend," she mused.

"He said Maxmillan knew he kept tabs on the women he spent time with. It was a game between the husband and wife." He shook his head. "I don't get it."

"Me either." Shandra put down her glass. "Who has the money in the marriage?"

Ryan studied his wife. Sometimes her questions or comments made him realize how lucky he was to have her as his partner in life. "That's a good question. One would think, the husband as he is the one laundering money, but you asked a valid question. One I hope Cathleen can answer for us."

The desserts arrived. Cinnamon laced apple pie with a mound of ice cream drizzled with a thick, rich caramel sauce. Shandra's favorite flavor was caramel. He'd known she would order this dessert as soon as he saw it on the menu. And it was a delicious choice.

The waitress handed the Maxmillan's the check tray.

Ryan slowly finished his dessert, watching as the woman paid the check and the couple, along with Springer, walked out of the restaurant.

Shandra licked her lips and wiped her face. "Do you think they'll go to their room?"

"They're staying in the penthouse suite across from Doring." He paid their check and helped Shandra out of the booth. "Let's check the bar first. They may have decided to go there rather than straight back to their room."

They walked out of the restaurant and down the lobby to the bar. One step inside and it was obvious the Maxmillan's were here. The three servers were talking to the couple. Springer stood at the bar, watching. His gaze met Ryan's.

"Go get us a table. I'll get drinks from the bar," he told Shandra and walked to the bar, standing beside Springer.

"You're working overtime," Springer said.

"I always do when there's a murder to solve."

"Murder? How do you leap from allergic reaction to murder?" Springer picked up his drink and sipped.

"I have my reasons." Ryan nodded toward the man's employer. "Want to introduce me?"

Springer grinned. "No way. You're on your own. I don't approach the dragon lady unless I have good news.”

"What can I get ya?" the bartender asked.

"A cup of hot tea and a cup of coffee." Ryan had a feeling it would be a long night and Shandra would appreciate the hot liquid before driving home.

The bartender gave him a disgruntled look and picked up two mugs.

"You do take your job seriously," Springer said, before picking up his drink and walking over to a table where he could keep an eye on his boss.

The bartender brought the two mugs over to Ryan. He paid and carried them to the table Shandra had chosen close to the Maxmillans.

"Are you planning on eavesdropping?" Ryan asked quietly, as he placed the tea in front of her.

She smiled. "You know me. I like to learn all I can."

He chuckled and placed his coffee on the table. "No time like the present to approach them." Ryan walked over to the tall table where the couple sat. Tabor Maxmillan had a face too pretty for a man. There wasn't a strong jawline, square chin, or even a manly nose. His features were dainty. His dark eyes were hidden behind long dark lashes. Even his lips had the bow shape his sisters had talked about growing up. "Mr. Maxmillan, I'm Weippe County Detective Greer. I'm investigating the death of a woman here in the lodge."

The man's eyelids lowered even more to hide his eyes completely. "Really? A death here? What does that have to do with me?"

The woman next to him cleared her throat.

"Or us?" he added.

Ryan shifted his gaze to the woman. She could have been a magazine model with her high cheekbones, full lips and delicate neck and nose, but her blue eyes were as hard and cold as ice. No, he didn't see a shimmer of compassion in her attitude at all. "Mrs. Maxmillan, what can you tell me about Emma Wickes?"

"Emma?" Mr. Maxmillan asked, his lashes rising and his eyes widening in disbelief. "Emma was the person we heard about? The woman who died yesterday?"

The shock on his face couldn't have been faked. They, his wife and her investigator, had kept the news from him.

"Yes. Ms. Wickes died from an allergic reaction yesterday while in the spa," Ryan stood with his gaze on both the husband and wife.

"What does that have to do with us?" Mrs. Maxmillan asked. Irritation sparked in her eyes.

"I believe you knew the woman. I'm talking to everyone who knew her." Ryan shifted just enough to peer into the woman's eyes but still have a peripheral view of her husband. "Did you know about her allergy to bees?"

"Why should I? I barely knew the woman."

"You knew Emma?" Mr. Maxmillan asked, standing up and glaring at his wife. "Is that why she turned on me, because you tried to pay her off?"

"Sit down, Tabor, you're making a spectacle." Mrs. Maxmillan glared at Ryan. "I'd prefer to talk about this in our suite not out here in public."

Ryan backed up. "I can follow you to the suite."

She picked up her glass and stared at him.

"Tomorrow. Ten A.M." She waved a hand and Springer came over to the table.

"You heard Mrs. Maxmillan. She'll talk with you tomorrow morning at their suite." He made a move to take hold of Ryan's arm.

"I'll be there." He glanced from the wife to the husband and back to the wife. "And you both better be."

Chapter Thirteen

On the drive home, seeing Ryan's headlights behind her and wondering what had happened after they left the bar kept Shandra from falling asleep while driving home. As they'd stood to leave, Bailey had entered the bar, scanned the room, and took a seat on the far side, away from the Maxmillans. Ryan said, when he'd been dismissed by Mrs. Maxmillan, he'd witnessed the FBI agent enter and take a spot at the bar.

She wondered if they had all planned to meet at the bar and seeing Ryan had sat far away from one another or were they suspicious of one another over Emma's death?

The front porch lights and yellow glow of lamps inside gave Shandra the same welcoming feeling she'd had the first time she'd driven up to the house and property. The barn doors were open wide for her to park the Jeep inside. From her initial visit, she'd decided to use the barn as her garage since building one would change the aesthetic of the place more than the structure she'd had built for her art studio. That newest building had an apartment above, in hopes Lil would live there. But the contrary older woman lived in a room next to the tack room in the barn.

Lil stood by the barn doors when Shandra emerged from the Jeep. Sheba whined and nudged her with her wide, tri-colored head.

"Hi girl. Did you have fun with Lil and Lewis?" Shandra rubbed her dog's head between the ears as they walked to the open doors.

The lights from Ryan's vehicle flashed across them as he pulled in under the lean-to on the side of the barn. It had been Lil's parking spot for her old pickup, but now she pulled farther in under the lean-to. Ryan usually had his vehicle out of her way any time she wanted to go somewhere.

"Did you have a good dinner?" Lil asked.

"Yes. But the dessert was the best." Shandra's stomach rumbled with happiness. "It was hot apple pie with ice cream and caramel sauce."

"That sounds good. Where did you eat?"

Shandra helped Lil close the barn doors. "Huckleberry Lodge."

"That very expensive?" she asked, lingering by the doors rather than doing her usual disappearing act.

"The food costs more than any other place in Huckleberry, but it's worth paying more." She wanted to see what the woman was thinking, but the moon was half hidden behind clouds and the shadows of the barn hid Lil's face. "Why did you want to know?"

"Just thinkin'. Night." She disappeared into the darkness of the barn's shadow.

"What were you two talking about?" Ryan asked, walking up to her with his computer bag.

"Nothing important." At least not to him, but it definitely had been important to Lil.

They entered the house. Sheba bounded down the hall and stretched out on her favorite rug in front of the fireplace.

"I'm going to get ready for bed," Shandra said as Ryan placed his computer bag on the dining room table.

"I may be a while. I want to see what reports have come in on the case and see if Cathleen dug up anything." Ryan walked over and kissed her temple. "See you whenever I get to bed."

"Don't stay up so late you can't think straight tomorrow. Something tells me you'll need your wits about you with that Mrs. Maxmillan."

"Yeah, me too." Ryan watched Shandra walk into the bedroom before he pulled out his computer and headed into the kitchen for a beer while he waited for the computer to boot up.

Back at the dining room table, he pulled up all the files for this case. While they still weren't officially calling it a homicide, he'd discovered enough evidence to persuade the sheriff and the D.A. to call it as such.

He clicked on his email and a message from Sheila Rickman at the forensic lab with "pregnant" in the subject line had him clicking.

The report revealed the urine tested positive for HCG. This led to the subsequent examination of the uterus which contained fibrillose material that could be products of conception and there was a prominent ovarian corpus luteum. Which to Sheila meant the deceased had been around ten weeks pregnant.

The report also stated what Sheila had said about the preliminary findings. The deceased had an allergic reaction and went into anaphylaxis.

Still nothing that would definitively state the death wasn't an accident. But he knew it was homicide. There were too many things that added up to foul play. Her changing her mind about testifying and running from the FBI. The pregnancy. The fact she didn't have an epinephrine pen in her purse, something she was known to do. And all the people who had a good reason to want her out of their lives were at the Huckleberry Lodge the day the victim died.

He sent an email with a copy of the forensics report and his typed notes of all the interviews to Sheriff Oldham and the D.A. They had to see what he did. This was a homicide.

~*~

Ella, Grandmother, sat on a tree limb watching a child playing below. Shandra sat down on the limb beside her. "Who is that, Ella?" she asked. The old woman shook her head. They continued to watch as a wispy cloud in the shape of a woman reached out, touching the child. The sharp image of the child turned wispy, and they both disappeared.

Shandra snapped awake and sat up. The bedside lamp was still on. Ryan hadn't come to bed. A glance at the clock showed 2 a.m. She stood and slid her feet into her slippers.

In the great room, she found Ryan on the couch, one leg on the furniture, one foot on the floor. His blank laptop sat askew on his lap.

"Ryan? Ryan, come to bed," Shandra said, lifting the computer from his lap and placing it on the coffee table.

His eyes opened and he sat up. "Hey." He scrubbed his hands over his face and peered at her. "What time is it?"

"A little after two. I woke, and you weren't in bed." She led the way back to the bedroom, turning off lights as she went. "I hope you learned something by staying up so late."

Ryan stood on his side of the bed undressing. "I did. But I'll have a clearer mind if I tell you in the morning."

"I have a dream to tell you." They both crawled into bed, and Ryan turned off the light.

~*~

Over breakfast Ryan revealed what he'd read in the reports the night before. The results of the autopsy and the Maxmillans. "It seems that both Tabor and Marcia Maxmillan are independently wealthy on their own. Tabor is in the money laundering mainly as a hobby."

"Hobby?" Shandra studied her husband. "How could one make illegal activity a hobby?"

"It's not the only illegal thing he's done. There's a string of hobbies that he's managed to pay his way out of jail time." Ryan's tone didn't hide his contempt for the man.

"Do you think his fooling around with other women was another hobby?" Shandra didn't like to think that Emma had given her heart to a man who toyed with it.

"That's something I hope to learn from Trower. Though I'd think Springer would be less biased. However, he is loyal to the Maxmillans where Trower isn't." Ryan sipped his coffee.

"Do you think the FBI agent was in love with Emma? Any chance the baby could be his?" Shandra wanted to think the woman and child would have been loved if their lives hadn't been cut short.

"I do think he loved her, but I don't think she reciprocated. It's unlikely the baby was his." Ryan set his coffee down. "I honestly hope it wasn't because I have a feeling he would not let anything stop him from taking the life of the person who took Emma's and his child's."

Shandra set a plate of French toast in front of Ryan. "Revenge never solves anything."

"I agree. Unfortunately, the only way to get Trower's cooperation would be to tell him about the pregnancy. I also want to see if he can get me all the surveillance they have on Ms. Wickes. She had to go to a doctor at some point. Maybe she confided in someone there."

"What about Bailey?" Shandra asked.

Ryan stared at her. "Do you really think Emma would have confided in the person guarding her?" He scoffed. "And Ms. Ullrich didn't seem like the sympathetic type."

"Truuue. But sometimes the strangest things will make a woman go mushy. Maybe the talk of a baby did that for her? I think I'll go to the lodge today and try and talk to her." She put a hand up. "I won't say anything about what we've learned other than the baby."

"You know I don't like you getting caught up in my investigations." Ryan put his fork down and spun on the stool to face her. "There is no need for you to put yourself in danger."

"I'm not putting myself in danger. I'm just visiting with someone who knew the woman I found dead on a massage table."

Chapter Fourteen

Shandra walked into the Huckleberry Lodge and straight to the elevator. She knew which room Bailey was staying in and thought it would be more spontaneous to just knock on her door than to call up and see if she was in.

The man who'd hung around the Maxmillan's table the night before stepped onto the elevator behind Shandra right before the doors closed. He smiled but it didn't engage his eyes.

"Looks like we're going to the same floor," he said, glancing at the panel of buttons.

"If you say so," she said, not sure whether to bring up knowing who he was.

"I understand you're the wife of the detective trying to make an accident a murder." His eyes bore into her.

"If you're talking about Detective Greer, yes, he's my husband. The other, I don't know anything about."

She shifted her gaze to the doors as the elevator dinged. Since the man had come in behind her, she waited for him to leave the elevator. When he lingered, she stepped out. He was waiting to see where she was going. Had he seen her in the lobby and decided to follow?

She walked down the hall, spotted a maid cleaning a room and turned around. "Looks like the person I came to see must be out." She quickly stepped back on the elevator and punched the button for the doors to close.

The elevator moved upwards and that's when she saw the lit number. She was headed to the top floor and the penthouses.

~*~

Ryan had phoned Trower first thing and asked him to come to the Huckleberry Police Station. It was better to question him away from the eyes of the Maxmillan's people.

They sat in the breakroom. Ryan wanted the man to know he wasn't a suspect. Hazel had brought them both coffee and set a plate of coffee cake in the center of the table.

"I'm not sure what more you can find out from me," Trower said, picking up the coffee and sniffing. He sipped. Surprise widened his eyes. "This is good. Most police stations have crappy coffee."

Ryan nodded toward the door. "It's why they keep Hazel around. She brews a mean cup of coffee, and you might want to try her cake, too." Ryan cut a piece and placed it on a napkin. He found plastic forks and handed one to Trower who was cutting a piece of cake.

"I was hoping you could help me get a copy of the

surveillance tapes the FBI has on Ms. Wickes." He put a bite of cake in his mouth, waiting for the agent to think about his request.

"What do you think the surveillance tapes will tell you?" Trower put a bite of the cake in his mouth. He chewed, swallowed, and said, "This tastes like something my mom made."

"The forensic report said she was ten weeks pregnant."

The man's facial expression hardened. "If you want to know what doctor she saw, it was Dr. Muriel Nartha at the Red Rock Medical Center."

"How do you know this?" Ryan sipped his coffee, watching the man over the rim of his cup.

"I was tailing her that day." Trower shoved his coffee and cake to the center of the table. "That's the day I figured out she was going to have Maxmillan's baby. I'm the one who suggested she turn against him because he wasn't going to claim the baby and would never marry her." He placed his elbows on the table and leaned forward. "It was her idea that telling Maxmillan she was pregnant with his baby would make him leave his wife." He pressed his back against the chair. "Have you seen Marcia Maxmillan? That's a woman who doesn't let anything get taken from her."

Ryan latched onto this bit of information. "Do you think she knew about her husband fathering a child with Ms. Wickes?"

"You've talked to her 'investigator'. He was dogging Emma just like we were. And I'm pretty sure it wasn't because Marcia was worried about Emma giving evidence against her darling Tabor. She'd bailed him out before and wasn't above bribing whoever she needed to do it again. But a pretty young woman and giving Tabor an heir…That I don't think Marcia would tolerate. If there were children to inherit, she would want those to be her children."

"Why haven't they had children? The Maxmillans?" Ryan asked.

"I'm not sure, other than as frosty as she is, I think that's why Tabor looks for other women. I think he's scared of his own wife." That last statement put a smile on the agent's face.

"You think he was bedding other women to prove he was a man because he couldn't 'get it up' for his overpowering wife?" Ryan had heard of such a thing happening.

Trower shrugged and pulled the cake and coffee back toward him. "Other than he is a thrill seeker, which I believe is why he married Marcia. Probably had a hell of a chase to get her to the alter. Then once he caught her, he didn't know what to do with her, so they both go their own ways."

"Would you still try to get the surveillance tapes for me?" Ryan asked, putting the last bite of the cake in his mouth.

"Sure. I can ask." His expression softened. "I think it would be the least the FBI could do since it is partly our fault Emma is dead. If we'd not let her get away, she'd still be safe."

~*~

Stepping off the elevator, Shandra stared at Sydney Doring's penthouse door. She didn't need him coming out and finding her here. They had a precarious relationship. She despised him, and he loathed her. He owned the lodge and thought he was God's gift to women. When the police thought she'd murdered his wife, she'd thought he had. She and Ryan both disliked the Lodge owner. During his wife's murder investigation and then later when Shandra's ex-lover had wound up dead on the ski slope and Sydney had been sleeping with one of the suspects, he'd pretty much thrown Ryan and Shandra out of the lodge.

If he found her here asking questions about another murder that had happened in his lodge, she was pretty sure she'd be barred for life.

The door on the other penthouse suite opened. It was Tabor Maxmillan. Shandra faced the elevator doors, as if waiting for them to open.

The man walked up beside her. He smelled good. Some earthy, rich cologne.

"Were you coming to see Marcia?" he asked.

Shandra flinched and glanced sideways. "No, I'm trying to get away from Sydney."

The man's jovial smile straightened. "In that case, let me help." He reached around her and punched a button. The doors opened and they stepped in.

"You're not a fan of Sydney's either?" she asked.

"No. I'm not. He upset someone I cared about."

The sorrow in the man's eyes had Shandra thinking he didn't have anything to do with Emma's death. He had loved her and probably the baby. She wondered about his marriage.

"Was it a woman? He is such a lecherous jerk." Shandra leaned her back against the wall of the elevator.

Tabor reached out and stopped the car halfway between the first and second floor. He put his hands on either side of her shoulders and his dark eyes bore into hers. "I know you're the wife of the detective investigating Emma's death. I saw you with him at the bar last night. You tell him to meet me…" He stepped back and ran a hand through his hair, making the longish locks stick out like matted fur on a much-loved teddy bear. "Where would be a place my wife wouldn't go that I could meet with your husband? I don't want to go to the police station."

Shandra had an idea. "Does she like donuts?"

Chapter Fifteen

Ryan sat in Daily Donut sipping coffee and reading a paper, waiting for Maxmillan to arrive. He couldn't believe Shandra had put this meeting together. But he should have known she'd get mixed up in the investigation more than he wanted.

The door jingled. He glanced over and raised the paper. It was Lil, pushing a man in a wheelchair. Was this her new friend? The one she wanted him to do a background check on? He waited until they'd ordered and sat, luckily with her back to him.

He lowered the paper and studied the man across the table from Lil. He was in his sixties, maybe even seventies. He had a full head of white hair and a white mustache. He was fit for being in a wheelchair. They seemed to be talking amicably.

The door jingled, and Maxmillan walked in. He spotted Ryan, but walked up to the counter and ordered.

Ryan folded the paper and watched the man as he

walked over to the table.

Maxmillan sat across from him, sipped his coffee, and waited.

"You asked to meet me, what did you want to say?" Ryan finally said, opening up the notepad he had sitting on the table.

The man set his coffee down and stared at Ryan. "I didn't kill Emma. I loved her. I know her going to the FBI was just her way of trying to get me to do what I should have done years ago, divorce my wife." He leaned back in his chair. "Unfortunately, I have nerves of steel to play tag with the cops in illegal activities, but I haven't the balls to go against my wife. A woman I loathe."

"Did she know Emma was pregnant with your child?" Ryan asked, watching the man.

Sorrow flashed in his eyes. His Adam's apple bobbed several times before he said in a cracking voice, "I do believe she found out about the baby. She already knew how much I cared about Emma. I'd been feeling Marcia out about leaving her."

Ryan stared at the man. He looked like a little boy who had broken a cherished object and didn't know how to fess up. "Why didn't you just pay an expensive attorney and get a divorce?"

"If only I could have. I didn't think Marcia and I would last this long. But now, if I divorce her, she'll take everything that I came into the marriage with and leave me with only my illegal operations." He smiled ruefully. "Without that money or hers, I can't fight the charges that could, and most likely would, be thrown at me." He laughed bitterly. "It's either prison with Marcia or prison with a thousand men. And she knows I could not survive around only men.

"I was trying to work out deals to hide some of my money from her before I told her I was leaving. But that damn Springer caught wind of it." The man's eyes heated with anger. "Ever since he came to work for Marcia, I haven't been able to get away with anything." He picked up the coffee. "And the worst part, I think they are trying to frame me for Emma's death."

Ryan stared at the man. "How?"

"I heard them whispering last night after you left the bar. They thought I was flirting with a bar maid, but I was listening to them. They said something about an epinephrine pen and hiding. I figured Springer must have taken Emma's pen from her belongings and plan to have it discovered in my things."

This explained why the man wanted to talk to him. He wanted to let Ryan know that he was being set up. Or he was the killer and was trying to make sure evidence that was connected to him would be consider invalid.

"What did you know about Ms. Wickes allergy?"

"She was afraid of bees. She showed me the pen thing she kept in her purse and how to use it. She told me if she ever got stung to use it immediately that was how allergic she was to bees." He shook his head. "Is that what caused her death? A bee sting?"

Ryan didn't want to give out what they knew, but he needed to gather information about the woman's allergy. "Forensics couldn't find a mark on her from a bee, but she died from an allergic reaction."

Maxmillan's eyes narrowed. "It wasn't a bee sting, but it was an allergic reaction?"

"What does that tell you?" Ryan asked. He could

see the man was putting things together in his head.

"I know for a fact Marcia has been working on a business deal with a natural makeup company and one of their products has a face cream with bee venom in it." Maxmillan shot to his feet. "You may have two murders on your hands after I talk to my wife."

"Sit," Ryan ordered. "You charging in and accusing her isn't going to help us make our case against her. What is the name of the company?" He held his pen over his notepad.

The man shook his head. "I don't know. She stays out of my business and I stay out of hers."

"Find out the name of the company. I'll make inquiries. In the meantime…" Ryan handed him a card. "Give me a call when you find out the company and if you overhear or see anything that might help in this investigation." He didn't believe for a minute Maxmillan was innocent, but maybe if the husband and wife were working against one another, he'd discover what really happened.

Maxmillan glanced at the card and nodded, before he walked out of the bakery.

Ryan rose to leave, started for the door, and spun around. He walked over to the table where Lil and the man sat. "Hi Lil." He nodded to the man.

Lil's expression remained smiling, but her face darkened. "What are you doing here?"

"Introducing myself to your friend." Ryan held his hand out. "Ryan Greer. Lil works for my wife."

The man grasped his hand with a strong grip and smiled. "Harvey Beatty. A friend of Lil's. Care to sit down and join us?"

From the expression on Lil's face, Ryan would

have loved to have sat down, just to annoy the woman, but he had work to do. "Some other time. I have to get back to work."

Ryan walked out of the Daily Donut thinking he needed to have Catherine pull up whatever she could find on Harvey Beatty, and he needed to set up an interview with Marcia Maxmillan.

Chapter Sixteen

After dodging the investigator and setting up the meeting between Ryan and Tabor, Shandra decided the only way she'd get to talk to Bailey without the investigator knowing was to call and ask her to meet.

Sitting at Ruthie's Diner, Shandra watched the people coming and going, hoping the woman would show. She'd been hesitant to talk to Shandra.

"Are you sure I can't get you a caramel shake?" Ruthie asked for the third time.

Shandra had refused not wanting to have the shake go warm as she talked to Bailey. But every time Ruthie asked, her mouth watered. "Just make it a small one. I'm meeting someone and don't want to waste it if it gets warm."

Her friend smiled. "Coming right up, and if I see someone come in before I bring it to you, I'll put it in the freezer."

"That's why you are my best friend." Shandra felt

lucky she had such a wonderful friend. Growing up she'd not had any best friends. Her stepfather had insisted she keep her Native American side hidden. Trying to not let people know who she really was made it hard to get close to anyone. Now she had nothing to hide from anyone and loved that she not only had Ruthie but Naomi and Miranda as close friends.

The bell over the door jingled. She glanced over.

Bailey stood in the door, scanning the diner. When her gaze landed on Shandra, she walked over and slid into the seat across the table. "Why did you need to talk to me here, and why are *you* talking to me? You're married to the investigating officer."

Shandra shrugged. "Anything you say to me doesn't go on any record. Since you and Emma were friends—"

Bailey snorted. "You know by now we weren't friends. I was paid to keep an eye on her. She was too naïve for me to be friends with."

Ruthie arrived. She placed an ice water in front of Bailey. "Can I get you anything?"

"This will be fine. I'm not staying long," Bailey said.

Ruthie raised her eyebrows and retreated.

Shandra decided she might as well get to the point and then let Ryan have a go at the woman. "Did you know that Emma was pregnant?"

The woman stared at her fingers, clutching the water glass. "I knew something like that might be the case. She asked to come here and then she said she wanted to see her family. I wasn't sure why all of a sudden she was so keen on that. Then I saw the prenatal vitamins in her bag. Didn't take long to put two and two together."

"Did you know who the father was?" Shandra tried to sound as if she didn't know.

The woman stared at her. "You're kidding right? Everyone who works for the Maxmillan's knew who the father was."

"And who besides Marcia didn't like that?" Shandra was trying to gauge if Bailey had a thing for her boss, Tabor.

The woman's jaw twitched as she clamped her teeth shut. Perhaps to keep from saying something.

"Do you work for Mr. or Mrs. Maxmillan?" That was a safe question.

"I work for Tabor. I don't think I could keep from killing Marcia if I worked for her."

The contempt in her voice gave Shandra more to think about. "Yet, that investigator of hers seems to get along well with both of them."

Another unladylike snort from Bailey. "That parasite knows what to do to stay on their good sides. I have more principles than he does."

Shandra wondered about those principals if she was keeping an eye on a woman who came up murdered. "And what exactly were you supposed to do while watching Emma?"

"Just keep her away from the cops, make her happy. That was Tabor's instructions. Keep Emma happy until I can talk to her." Bailey stared at the napkin she was picking to pieces. "That's why I let her go to the coffee shop alone. She said she needed some time without me hovering over her to think." She shrugged. "I thought maybe she was thinking of a way to say good-bye to Tabor when he arrived—"

"Did Emma know Tabor was coming here? To talk to her?" Shandra wondered if that was why she was so upset to see her cousin working here.

"Yes, I'd told her that morning. After I reported to him where we were, he said he'd find a way to get here. Only he showed up with Marcia in tow. We were trying to figure out a way for him and Emma to meet without Marcia knowing." Bailey sighed. "But that dragon knows everything. I think she has a crystal ball."

"Or a loyal group of people who tell her everything," Shandra said.

"More like greedy bastards who would turn on their own to make money."

That must be the principals she'd talked about. "Someone said they saw you in the spa the day of Emma's death. You told Ryan and I that you didn't know she was in there."

The woman blushed. "I went looking for her. After asking around I discovered she'd been talking to someone from the spa. I spotted a person in a white shirt go in a locked door. I used my skills and went in. I saw Emma sitting in what looked like a break room. She said her cousin offered to give her a massage, and she thought it would help her think. I left and went back to the room. Then you and the detective showed up, and I said what I thought would keep me out of the whole thing." She glared at Shandra. "Obviously it didn't."

"How did Emma look?"

"Not like she was going to die any minute."

"Did you see anyone you knew?"

"No, only Emma." Bailey slid out of the booth. "That's all I know. And if your husband comes to get my statement, it will sound the same." She strode to the door and out onto the sidewalk.

Ruthie appeared at the end of the table with a frosty caramel shake. "That was one interesting lady."

Shandra nodded her head. "Thanks for keeping the shake cold." She dipped the long-handled spoon into the ice cream and savored the first bite. Cold. It reminded her of the woman she'd just talked to.

Halfway through the shake, the door jingled. Marcia Maxmillan's investigator walked in. Had he been following Bailey? Did he know they'd talked? She pulled her gaze from him and focused on the shake.

Footsteps approached. The investigator slid onto the bench where Bailey had sat. "That looks good." He raised a hand, drawing Ruthie's attention.

When her friend arrived at the table, he pointed to the shake. "I'll have what she's having."

Ruthie glanced at Shandra and then hurried to the counter.

"I saw you and Bailey talking. Anything I need to know about?"

"Nope. We were discussing the weather, the quaintness of this place." Shandra moved her arm as if showing off the décor.

The man laughed. "I caught you headed to her room at the lodge, and now I found the two of you together here. What lies is she telling you?"

"Lies? What kind of lies do you think she's spreading?" Shandra sipped on her shake, now that it was soft enough to draw it up through the straw, and waited.

The man was clearly deciding how to deal with her. The truth or a fabrication. She had no doubt that he would lie to his grandmother if it kept him in the graces of Marcia Maxmillan.

"Bailey has the idea that one of these days she'll become Mrs. Tabor Maxmillan. But I can guarantee you, that will never happen."

"She didn't give me that impression." While she had registered Bailey's interest in her boss, Shandra wasn't about to give the man any information on anyone.

"She's a cool one. But when she thinks people aren't looking, she practically drools over her boss." The man leaned back as Ruthie arrived with his shake.

"Thank you, Ruthie," Shandra said, knowing full well the man wasn't going to appreciate anything someone did for him.

"Why are you following me?" Shandra asked.

"I'm not following you." He didn't look at her. He stuck the spoon into the shake and slipped the bite into his mouth.

"At the lodge, I know you followed me up to the fourth floor to see who I was visiting. And now, it feels as if you followed me here."

He shook his head. "I'm keeping track of Bailey, who, came to see you here. Back on the subject. Why did she come see you?"

"I was here, she came in, and I figured we didn't need to both sit alone." She hated not telling the truth, but this man could have killed Emma. He worked for a woman who wanted Emma out of her husband's life.

"Were you in the spa the day Emma died?" she decided to not let him ask all the questions.

"No."

That was quick. "Where were you?"

"With Marcia. She and I were going over our plan

to keep Tabor and Emma apart."
She stared at him. "Forever?"

Chapter Seventeen

After several hours of putting all the suspects' movements in chronologic order, Ryan wasn't any closer to knowing who could have killed the victim. Shandra had called and told him that Ms. Ullrich had admitted to seeing Emma in the breakroom. Which quite possibly made her the last person other than the killer to see the victim alive. Or she was the killer. Had she somehow got Emma to drink something with honey?

But who would have had access to the honey beforehand and would have known Ms. Wickes would be in the spa area? Her visit there seemed to have been a spur of the moment thing.

He'd collected all of the raw honey from the spa and had a deputy digging through the trash bins to see if a jar had been thrown out. She had to have ingested the venom since Forensics hadn't found any sting sites.

Unless Maxmillan's belief his wife had her killed

and used the bee venom cream from the cosmetic company she had just acquired. He'd put Catherine on that as soon as he'd walked out the bakery's door. And she'd sent him the name of the company and that Mrs. Maxmillan had purchased it a month ago. Plenty of time for her to get her hands on a jar of the cream that would kill her husband's lover and love child.

Shandra wasn't going to like that he still hadn't checked Valerie off his list of suspects. He looked up Ms. Wickes' parents' address and headed to his vehicle. He wanted to know more about the family dynamics. Right now, Valerie Howe was still at the top of his list. She had means and opportunity. It was the motive that was escaping him.

~*~

At the Wickes residence Ryan introduced himself and followed the forlorn Mr. Wickes into the living room.

"I don't understand why you are talking to us. We didn't even know our Emma was back in Idaho," the older man said, dropping into a recliner that looked like one more drop might make it fold.

"I understand Emma left here and went to Las Vegas to dance. Was she good?" Ryan asked.

The man shoved back up to his feet and headed out of the room. "Come with me."

Ryan followed the slightly hunched man down a narrow hall to what looked like a bedroom door.

"If Geraldine were here, we couldn't look." Mr. Wickes opened the door and a room bursting with pink and ruffles met their gazes. "This was Emma's room." The man stepped inside and waved to a wall of framed pictures and shelves of awards. "Emma was the best dancer to ever come out of these parts.”

A young Emma stood on point in a white tutu in one photo and was dressed in a bright blue swing dress in another. The photos depicted every recital the girl had performed.

“Did she get a dancing job in Vegas?” Ryan asked, thinking if the girl had talent how did she end up with the likes of Tabor Maxmillan.

“She was dancing in one of the big casino’s dance troupe, then she sent a letter saying she’d got a job as an assistant to a rich man and could make more money as an assistant and it was easier on her body.” He shook his head. “Then we didn’t hear from her for over a year. That was after Geraldine had a heated discussion that if she was making that kind of money she was doing more than an assistant. They quarreled and that was the last we heard from Emma.”

“How close were Emma and Valerie?”

“Valerie Howe, her cousin?” the man seemed puzzled.

“Yes. Were they confidantes as young girls or women?” Ryan had to figure out if there was something that had been nagging at Valerie all these years.

Mr. Wickes pointed to a photo. His finger was under a face in the back row. “That’s Valerie. She was always heavy on her feet and made a funny face when she was concentrating so the dance instructor always put her in the back row.” He led Ryan out of the room. “I never heard or seen the two girls giggling or carrying on when they were together. They were both pretty quiet.”

“Did they hang out together a lot?” Ryan wasn’t sure if this would help him get any closer to the truth but knowing the relationship between the cousins had to get him somewhere.

"No. They were only a year apart, but about the only time I saw them together were family gatherings and the recitals. I don't know how they got along at dance classes. You'd have to ask Geraldine or Valerie's mother." Mr. Wickes dropped into the recliner again, making the chair twang.

"Thank you for your time." Ryan headed for the front door. The man didn't make any motions to show him out.

Standing by his vehicle, Ryan wondered if a trip to see Valerie's parents would help. According to the address he had, they weren't that far out of his way as he drove home. As much as he'd love to pin the murder on the Maxmillans and their entourage of people, the evidence was pointing at family.

~*~

Shandra stopped in at Dimensions Gallery before heading home. She wanted to remind Naomi and Ted that she would be bringing in a new vase the following week.

As she opened the door to enter the gallery a man in his late sixties or early seventies, rolled toward her. It was hard to tell his age since he was sitting in a wheelchair, but his upper body looked muscular for his shock of white hair.

"Excuse me," he said.

"No problem." Shandra held the door open and the man rolled out onto the sidewalk. He turned right and headed down the sidewalk faster than a person could walk.

Naomi popped out from behind a display. "Oh, I

thought it was Harvey leaving that caused the door to buzz." She walked to the door and locked it. "He has a fondness for your work."

"Really?" Shandra stared behind her but didn't see the man in the wheelchair.

"Yes. He's been in here several times the last month looking around and just sitting, admiring your work." Naomi led the way to the back of the gallery.

"Well, that's good. Then you'll have space for the vase I'm bringing in next week." Shandra walked alongside Naomi. The couple lived on the second floor of the building. The stairs were in the back room where they packed and unpacked the art they purchased and sent to people.

Her friend flipped the switch to the gallery lights and led her into the backroom. "You finished the piece you were telling me about? I can't wait to see it!"

"It's cooling then I have to decide if I'm going to put on wax or glaze. I love the carbon pattern left from the horse hair I draped over the vase. It almost looks like an ancient etching on a cave wall." Shandra had been proud of the vase she'd finished this week. It had an ethereal feeling to it that she knew would call to many people's hearts.

"Wow! Just describing it, I'm fascinated to see it." Naomi stopped at the bottom of the stairs. "Want to come up for dinner? Ted ran to Rigatoni's."

"Not tonight, but thank you." Shandra headed to the back door.

"Did you get caught up in the death at the lodge?" her friend asked.

Shandra stopped, her hand on the door knob. "I was one of the people who found the body."

"No! And I suppose you are up to your eyeballs in the investigation right alongside Ryan."

Shandra didn't understand why Naomi's tone felt like she was scolding. "I was there, so I'm a witness, not a suspect."

"I meant, you always put yourself in danger. There are more people these days who care about you and would be devastated if anything happened to you." Naomi wiggled her ring finger. "You have a husband who cares about you. How do you think he'll feel if you get hurt or worse because you were helping him?"

She shook her head. "It's not like that at all. Most people think it was an accidental death."

"But it's not?"

A groaned escaped before she caught it. "Don't tell anyone, but Ryan and I are pretty sure it wasn't an accident."

The back door pulled from her hand and she stepped back.

Ted walked through the door.

Her stomach grumbled at the aroma of spicy tomato sauce and cheese.

"You sure you don't want to stay for dinner?" Naomi asked, this time smiling, knowing Shandra loved anything that was cooked at the Rigatoni Restaurant.

"I could call Ryan and see if he'll be home for dinner."

Chapter Eighteen

The monitor light glared at Ryan as he scrolled through the documents on the Wickes case. Shandra had called him two hours ago to see where he was and if he minded that she stayed in town to have dinner with Ted and Naomi.

He preferred her hanging out with her friends than running around trying to help him solve this case. There was a killer in Huckleberry, and he wasn't sure if it was a woman who had lived here her whole life or the group from Las Vegas.

The way his victim died had been planned. It sounded as if no one in the victim's family had known she was even in the state. But all of the people who had an interest in what she was doing and who she was talking to, knew where she was.

What bothered him the most—the spa had been a spur of the moment thing. How had the killer known to find her there and administer what had to have been bee venom? He was still waiting for a report on all the honey jars he and the deputy had collected to see if any had an unusual amount of bee venom in them. The glasses he'd bagged from the room next to the murder site had fingerprints from Alice, the spa manager, and Chad, the man who worked in the reception area. It turned out he also gave massages. The two had said they were discussing his schedule in that room earlier in the day because it was not being used.

This was strange considering Alice had an office, but he wasn't going to worry about the relationships between the spa workers. It didn't have anything to do with the murder. The pregnancy had changed Ms. Wickes plans. Had it also changed Maxmillan's or possibly his wife's?

Until more tests came back, he could track down more of the whereabouts of the people involved.

Ryan's mind and body snapped to attention. Surveillance tapes and the readouts from the keycards of the people at the lodge. He wrote up a warrant for the tapes and key activity and sent it off to the district attorney. If he was lucky the D.A. would see it first thing in the morning and he'd have the papers in his hand by nine and head to the lodge.

~*~

Ted walked down to the back door with Shandra. "Tough break for the Wickes family," he said.

She stopped and stared at him. "Did you know Emma?"

He shook his head. "I was friends with her brother. He was fifteen years older than Emma. He died in the service."

"Were they the only two children?" she asked, now

123

understanding the bedroom left as a shrine. Ryan had told her about the photos and awards.

"Yes. After Rory died, Mr. and Mrs. Wickes poured everything they had into Emma. Their hearts broke when she moved to Las Vegas. In a way, you couldn't help but think it was the best thing for her to do. Her parents had become overprotective. Monitoring her actions all the time. Emma didn't have a moment's peace."

"Did you stay in contact with the Wickes?" Shandra wondered if they would have been excited to have a grandchild even if the father disowned it, or if they would have felt Emma had tarnished the family name?

"I haven't seen much of them since Rory died. I've mostly heard about Emma and how she was treated from a cousin."

"Valerie? Valerie Howe?" Shandra asked, not sure she wanted to know.

Ted stared at her. "No. My cousin Rachel. She was friends with Emma."

A thought struck. "Would your cousin be someone Emma would have confided in?"

"Confided? What do you mean?" He leaned against the wall, crossing his arms.

"Just confided. Were they that close?" Shandra wondered if Emma had told her friend about Tabor and any plans they may have made.

"I don't know. You'd have to give her a call." He pulled his cell phone from his pocket and scrolled through the numbers. He tapped and her phone jingled. "I sent you her number. I don't think she'll know anything, but you can talk to her. Christ! We'll have to go to the funeral or Rachel will be on my back." Ted opened the back door.

Shandra knew when to leave. While Naomi would have stood there talking for hours, her husband preferred to get work done over talking. That was why he took care of the paperwork and money and Naomi charmed the buyers.

She walked down the alley to the side street. The sun had set as she'd entered the gallery. The streetlights lit her way back to her Jeep. She hadn't called Lil to tell her she was running late. Once inside the vehicle, Shandra pulled out her phone and hit the speed dial for Lil.

The phone rang until an automated voicemail came on. Which wouldn't do any good. Lil didn't know how to do anything with her phone other than answer it and dial. A quick check of the time and Shandra figured Lil was taking a shower. While the eccentric woman wouldn't live in the apartment over the studio, she used the bathroom.

Before pulling away from the curb, Shandra texted Ryan. *Are you home?*

Getting ready to head that direction.

Me, too. See you there. Shandra tucked her phone in her purse and headed down the street to County Road 15.

~*~

Ryan caught up to Shandra about twenty miles from town. He followed far enough back that his headlights wouldn't shine bright in her mirrors. That was a long dinner with the Nortons. He wondered what they'd talked about. Art or the death at the lodge. He shook his head, most likely the later.

His phone buzzed. He pulled over to the side of the road to dig it out of the leather holster on his belt. It was the forensics lab in Coeur d'Alene.

"Greer," he answered.

"Detective Greer, this is Douglas at the State Forensics Lab. Sheila told me to contact you as soon as we had anything that might make your victim's death appear anything other than accidental."

Adrenaline had Ryan's heart pumping double time. "And?"

"We combed short dark hairs out of the victim's hair. We ran them for type. They came back human. I found one that might have enough follicle to get a DNA match. I'll keep you posted on that."

"You said one might have follicle. Were the others broken? Or cut?"

"One end was split and the other was a clean cut. As if the person had just had a haircut," Douglas answered.

"Where were the hairs found in her hair? On a side, the back?" Ryan flashed the image of the body as he'd found it in his mind.

"That's the weird part. It was mostly in the very back of her head. Almost as if it had been placed there." The lab tech's voice sounded skeptical of the evidence.

Ryan thought the same thing. It wouldn't surprise him if the one with the follicle came back as Tabor Maxmillan. The man's belief he was being framed could be true. Or he could have set it up himself to claim he was being framed.

"Thank you. Send the report and let me know as soon as you find someone who matches the DNA."

Ryan flicked his finger across the screen and

noticed lights coming up behind him fast. He waited for the vehicle to go by. It was Lil in her old pickup. He didn't think she drove over 45 miles per hour at any given time. She'd gone by him going at least 60.

He pulled onto the county road and drove the speed limit of 55. He knew where to find her and ask why she was driving so fast at night when animals could leap out into the road in front of her.

Chapter Nineteen

The Jeep's headlights slid across the dark log house and closed doors of the barn as Shandra drove into the open meadow where the house, studio, and barn sat.

Where was Lil?

Now she was getting worried. First, she didn't answer her phone and now it appeared as if the woman wasn't even here. Or was laying somewhere hurt. It wouldn't be the first time she'd discovered her employee and friend in need of medical care.

Shandra parked the Jeep in front of the barn doors. "Lil! Sheba!"

Whining and a mournful howl came from inside the barn. Shandra hurried to the doors, flung them open, and was nearly flattened by two big paws planted on her chest.

She ruffled the dog's fur on the sides of her head. "Where's Lil?"

The sound of a vehicle, which she assumed was Ryan, rumbled behind her. Spinning around, she realized the rumble was Lil's old pickup. The vehicle shot out of the tree-lined driveway into the clearing and screeched to a stop before slowly rolling into her parking spot under the lean-to.

Shandra left her Jeep sitting where it was and walked over to the pickup's driver's side door, waiting for the woman to get out.

Lil opened her door as Ryan's work vehicle emerged from the treed drive and pulled in behind Lil's pickup.

"Where were you?" Shandra asked Lil. Even in the darkness she could see that the woman had on one of her nice set of clothes that she wore to weddings and funerals.

"I went to town for dinner." Lil spun on the heel of her best pair of cowboy boots and headed to the back door of the barn.

"What were you doing driving that fast at night?" Ryan asked from behind Shandra.

Lil spun around. "Whatcha doin'? Spyin' on me?"

"I was parked alongside the road taking a phone call when you flew by me like you were headed away from a fire." Ryan shifted his computer bag to his other shoulder. "Lil, you can't drive that fast at night. A deer or other animal could jump out into the road."

"I've lived here my whole life. I know what can jump out. I'm not a fool." Lil spun around and slammed into the barn.

Shandra faced Ryan. "I think something didn't go well."

"That's an understatement. Was she wearing

clothes that fit?"

"Yes. I think she had a date with this mystery man, Harvey." Shandra walked over to her Jeep and drove it into the barn.

Ryan helped her close the doors and they, along with a frolicking Sheba, walked to the house.

Inside, Shandra fed Sheba and walked into the kitchen. "Did you get anything to eat?"

"I had Blane grab me a burger from Ruthie's." Ryan set his computer bag on the counter. "How was your visit with Ted and Naomi?" He grabbed a beer out of the refrigerator.

Shandra filled the hot water pot and flicked the switch. "Good. Ted was best friends with Emma's brother before he died."

Ryan stopped the bottle of beer halfway to his lips. "Emma had a brother? I didn't see any evidence of it at the house."

She told Ryan everything Ted had told her. "And he gave me his cousin Rachel's phone number." She held up her phone, showing Ryan the text. "Do you want to contact her?"

He pulled out his logbook and copied down the number. "I don't think it will help, but I won't turn down any possible help on this case."

"Is anything coming together?" she asked, pouring boiling water into a mug and tossing in a bag of herbal tea.

"Yes and no." He picked up his computer bag, beer, and log book, and wandered into the great room.

Shandra snagged a bag of chocolate with caramel bits cookies from the freezer and followed. The cookies had been one of her baking experiments that turned out to be one of her favorite cookies. She curled her legs onto the couch and sat beside Ryan.

"Any proof this is a homicide and not accidental?" she asked, knowing if he didn't come up with proof of homicide, the death would go down as accidental.

"We may have something besides my gut." He told her about the hair.

"You need to ask all the people involved when they last had a haircut." She tapped a frozen cookie against her bottom lip, thinking. "You know, the person who planted the hair might slip up and not hide their smugness that you believe the hair was from the killer."

"I'm glad you are on my side. You have a mind for criminal behavior." Ryan leaned over and kissed her head. "Thankfully you use it to help me and not kill people."

She shuddered at the thought of ending anyone's life. Being alive was a precious thing many didn't get to see all the way through. Her thoughts went to her father who had his life cut short by her stepfather. And Lil's first love. He'd been killed before the two of them could start a life. No, life was too precious to take from anyone.

"You went quiet. Did I misspeak?" Ryan put a hand on her thigh.

"No. I was just thinking how I could never take anyone's life from them. There are so many, like Emma, my dad, and Lil's lover, that never had a chance to live to an old age."

He pulled her into his arms. "As long as we keep putting away those who do take away others' lives, we'll have saved some from an untimely death."

She snuggled into his embrace. That was why she

now believed in Ella's dreams and her husband's intuition.

~*~

Shandra woke. It was still dark. Sheba was whimpering in her sleep on the dog bed and Ryan softly snored on his side of the bed. What had woke her? Both these sounds were usual every night.

A light flickered under the bedroom door.

She froze. Someone was in their house. Everyone knew Ryan was a policeman. She gently shook Ryan's arm and leaned close to whisper, "Someone is in the house."

He immediately sat up nearly knocking heads with her. "Where?" he whispered back.

She pointed to the door. A faint light swept under the door again.

Ryan put a hand on Shandra's chest. "Stay put." He slipped out of bed, pulled his Glock out of the holster on top of the dresser, and moved to the door.

Sheba started to stir. Before Ryan said anything, Shandra dropped to the floor beside her dog.

With the gun in one hand, he opened the bedroom door enough to scan the great room. Someone leaned over the dining room table, looking at his laptop. He snuck up behind the person.

Before he could tell the intruder to freeze, the person spun around, throwing a roundhouse kick. Ryan's gun flew out of his hand.

The intruder sprinted to the front door, throwing it open and disappearing.

Ryan ran to the door. He caught sight of the person's back disappearing down the lane. The intruder must have parked at the county road. Ryan sprinted to the bedroom, picked up his phone and called dispatch.

"This is Detective Greer. I had a break-in. Ask any cars out or near County Road Fifteen to look for a car speeding down the road. They are to apprehend and let me know."

By the time Ryan started a vehicle, the intruder would be long gone. And he had no idea which direction they would have driven. Though he had a pretty good idea it would have been to the Huckleberry Lodge.

"Did you see who it was?" The lights went on. Shandra stood by the light switch, her hand holding onto Sheba's collar.

"No. Only the body. Slender and the height of most of my suspects." Ryan walked by her to his slippers on the floor by the bed. He slipped his feet in and headed to the back door.

"Where are you going?" Shandra asked.

"To get my fingerprinting kit., Don't touch anything on or around the table, or the front door." He was pretty sure the person had on gloved. He wasn't sure what irked him more. That someone broke in or that they had the audacity to break into a policeman's home. Either way they had wanted to know what he knew pretty bad. And he was sure it had to do with the murder of Emma Wickes. closed the front door, locked it, which he knew he'd done before going to bed.

On the way to his pickup, he decided it was time to talk Shandra into a security system. With his line of work, it was a good idea. He never knew when someone he put in jail might get out and decide to take revenge.

"Man or woman?" Shandra asked, greeting him at

the back door with a cup of hot chocolate.

He studied her and by passed the drink to continue down the hall to the table where his computer sat. "What woman did you have in mind?"

"Not Valerie, if that's what you're thinking. And she isn't slender." Shandra carried two cups of cocoa to the table in front of the couch. "Did they take anything?"

"No. Whoever it was, wanted to know what we know." He walked over to his computer and hit the space bar. The computer came on. "Looks like we caught him or her before they accessed my computer." He was relieved to know information on the case hadn't been leaked by him. He began dusting the keys and lid for finger prints. Also the table top. Nothing. The person had worn gloves.

"I don't think the intruder will be back tonight. However, tomorrow we're installing a security system. There have been too many people getting into this house undetected. It's evident our large furry security system isn't working." He patted Sheba's head as he sat down on the couch to drink the cocoa.

Ryan put his weapon on the table before picking up the hot chocolate.

Shandra sat on the couch patting Sheba's head. "How can you just sit here drinking cocoa after that?"

He peered into her eyes. "I'm angry someone broke into our house. I'm happy he or she was only after information and not here to harm us." He picked up her hand. "I called it in and hope the person drove like a demon to get away and the deputies catch him." He sipped the hot drink she'd prepared for him. "I know whoever it was won't be back."

He motioned to her cup of chocolate. "Drink up. We both need sleep." He could be nonchalant on the outside for Shandra's sake, but he was boiling inside wanting to find out who the person was that invaded their privacy and had the balls to break-in to find out information about the investigation.

Chapter Twenty

Shandra sat at the shoreline of a lake. Grandmother was perched on a post at the dock. "What are we doing here Ella?" Grandmother's hand pointed farther along the shoreline. A woman with dark hair lay face down on a blanket on the bank. Someone leaned over the woman's back. It was hard to tell if it was a man or woman. All she could see were the bottoms of the second person's feet and a white robe. "Is that Emma? Who is that and what are they doing?" she asked, standing to walk toward the two.

A hand clutched her arm, holding her from getting closer. The person in the robe disappeared and the woman's body bloated like a grotesque balloon.

"That's the person who gave her bee venom." Shandra frantically looked for the person but all she saw was water and the body floating away.

"Shandra? Shandra. Wake up." Ryan's voice penetrated her dream.

She swam up out of the dream and stared into her husband's eyes. Quickly, before the scene whisked away like the person leaning over the woman, she told Ryan what she'd dreamt.

He pulled her into his arms. "I better dig into the company Maxmillan told me his wife owns. He said that the cream had bee venom in it."

"And Marcia would be at the top of my list considering what we've learned about Tabor's feelings for Emma and the child she was carrying."

"My thoughts, too."

They settled in to get another couple hours of sleep.

~*~

After Ryan headed to work, Shandra went out to the studio to put the final shine on her horse hair raku vase. After today the vase would be ready for delivery to Dimensions Gallery.

Shandra had the vase on the workbench, and Sheba had settled onto her bed under the bench.

The studio door opened and slammed shut. Lil stomped over to Shandra.

"A little cranky today?" Shandra asked. The woman was moodier than a cat.

"I don't want to talk about it. Do you need me to glaze those coasters?" She pointed to the box of fired coasters they'd taken out of the kiln before Shandra fired the three small vases she planned to glaze and send to a gallery in Jackson Hole Wyoming.

"That's a good idea. That way we'll be ahead in inventory when the stores start calling for the coasters in November." To help keep the money coming in steady, she'd talked the local souvenir shops in the area to carry coasters from her clay with Huckleberry Mountain etched on them. What had started as a small project now took up as much of Lil's time glazing, firing, and packaging them as it did Shandra's time cutting them out and etching.

Lil stomped over to the glazing bench and slid the box of fired coasters closer to her.

Shandra went back to waxing the vase. She knew when Lil was ready to talk, she'd start spilling what had happened the night before. From her foul mood, there was a pretty good chance it had to do with Harvey.

After forty-five minutes of Shandra rubbing the vase to a high shine, Lil cleared her throat.

"Sorry I wasn't here when you came home last night," she started.

"Don't worry about it. I forgot to call and let you know I had dinner with Ted and Naomi." Shandra glanced over her shoulder at the back of the woman.

"Ted and Naomi." Lil's voice was barely loud enough for Shandra to hear.

She wasn't sure if she should respond or the woman was just thinking.

"I had dinner with Harvey, the man I've been visiting with at the Daily Donut." Lil's voice was louder. "I'm sure Ryan told you he saw us at the bakery."

Shandra shifted, leaning her butt against the workbench and watching Lil. "No, Ryan didn't tell me he saw you at the bakery. I know you think he tells me everything he sees, he doesn't. He understands discretion."

Lil spun around and stared at her. "He didn't say anything about me and Harvey?"

"Not about seeing you, no." Shandra wasn't going to tell her friend she and Ryan had been looking into the man.

"Well, we went to dinner at Rigatoni's. It was easier for Harvey to wheel over there and meet me. Would have looked stupid if I used a piece of wood to wheel him up in the back of my pickup." She snorted. "That would have got tongues wagging."

Shandra chuckled at the picture Lil was painting. "That it would."

"Anyway, we had dinner. Miranda waited on us. I can see why you and her are friends." Lil dropped the brush covered in glaze in a jar of water. "Everything was going good until that no-account from over at the feed store walked by our table. He backtracked and started asking Harvey what he was doing having dinner with Huckleberry's certified crazy woman."

"Lil, I'm sorry. You know there are only a few people in Huckleberry who still think of you as crazy." Shandra knew there were more than a few given the woman's eccentric need to wear only purple clothing and tell everyone exactly what she thought, whether they wanted to know or not.

"Well, that lunatic made Harvey's eyes go big and round. When Claude left, Harvey said he wasn't hungry for dessert and really needed to get home, he was expecting a phone call." Her eyes glistened with unshed tears as she peered at Shandra. "He hadn't mentioned anything about needing to be home for a call before that lunatic Claude put on his show."

"I'm sure Harvey is smart enough to figure out Claude is the crazy one."

"I don't know. He couldn't get out of the restaurant

and away from me fast enough." She swiped at her nose with the sleeve of her purple sweatshirt. "I don't know whether to go to the Daily Donut and sit at our table and see if he shows or forget about him."

"You could give him a call," Shandra suggested. "See if he'll listen to you."

"I don't have a phone number for him. We made the date for dinner at the bakery." Lil put the lid on the glaze jar. "I think I'll go sit in my pickup a block or so away from the bakery. If he shows up at our usual time, I'll go in. If he doesn't, I'll know he believes Claude."

Not sure that was the best idea but knowing she wouldn't be able to talk the woman out of it, Shandra nodded. "Want me to come along?"

Lil studied her a moment. "No. I won't want to talk to anyone if he doesn't show up." With that she walked out of the studio and the roar of her pickup starting up revealed she was headed to town.

"Looks like it's you and me," Shandra said to Sheba, standing back and inspecting the vase she'd waxed.

~*~

Ryan asked at the lodge registration desk if Mrs. Maxmillan was in. The clerk assured him she was.

At the top floor, the elevator dinged and he stepped out as Sidney Doring had the door to the Maxmillan's penthouse close behind him.

"Detective Greer, what are you doing on this floor?' Doring always acted as if he were royalty but the only royalty he could claim would be a royal pain in the ass.

"I'm making inquiries about the woman who was found dead in your spa." Ryan rarely let Doring's attitude get to him. But he also didn't like the man. He'd struck Shandra when Ryan first met her and that had put Doring on the bottom rung of humanity.

"That woman dying wasn't my fault." Doring's voice rose an octave.

"Then you won't mind my asking questions to find out who did." Ryan moved Doring out from in front of the Maxmillan's door and knocked.

The door opened. "I told you we don't know—" Tabor Maxmillan's eyes widened at the sight of Ryan. "Sorry, I thought you were Doring." His gaze sliced beyond Ryan to the lodge owner. "Come in."

Ryan entered the penthouse. It had the same layout as the one Doring lived in but this one was more warmly decorated. "I have some questions for your wife. Is she in?'

"Marcia!" Maxmillan called.

"Why on earth are you…" the woman appeared through a room that must have been a bedroom. "Oh, I see." She coolly took a seat on the sofa. "What do you want to know?"

Ryan sat on the straight-backed chair facing the sofa. "I was wondering if you could tell me about the company you own that has a face cream with bee venom as one of the ingredients."

The woman flicked a glare at her husband before, smiling. "I purchased Glorious Aging about a month ago after having used their products and seeing what a difference they made. It is the height of the natural anti-aging agents like shale rock, shitake mushrooms, and bee venom." She stood. "I have some samples with me. Would you like to take one to your wife?"

Ryan motioned for the woman to sit back down.

"No. My wife is perfect just the way she is."

"I would have to agree if that was your wife with you in the lodge restaurant the other night. Such high cheekbones and beautiful coloring."

"How many containers of the product do you have with you that contain bee venom?" Ryan asked.

"The ones I use and a couple more." She patted her smooth cheeks.

"I need to know exactly how many you have, and if any are missing." Ryan stood. "How about you take me to the products."

Mrs. Maxmillan humphed, but stood and led him into the room she'd appeared from. "I have these three creams and this oil—" Her words cut off as she lifted the lid on a small bag. "I know I brought three jars of the cream with me." Her eyes narrowed. "I'll have the head of whoever took my cream. These jars are a new product not available on the market. I've been testing the product myself."

"Tabor!" she yelled, making Ryan back up from the loudness.

"You bellowed, Marcia?" Maxmillan asked, stepping into the room.

Ryan was slowly getting a better picture of the relationship between the husband and wife. Had a policeman arrived and followed Shandra into a bedroom, he would have been right beside her. That Maxmillan had stayed in the other room, even though he was the one who had told Ryan about the cream, showed him he hoped his wife was the murderer. His actions so far made Ryan think maybe he was framing his wife. Get rid of the pregnant lover and the wife all at the same time.

"Did you take one of my creams?" the woman accused her husband.

"I don't touch your youth seeking concoctions." Maxmillan leaned his shoulder against the door jamb as if he feared stepping into his wife's lair.

"Who besides us has been in this penthouse?" she ordered.

"Your lap dog, Lance. Sidney Doring. This detective. You and me." He snapped his fingers. "The maid. I'm sure she would be in need of a three-hundred-dollar jar of youth cream. She looked about nineteen."

"Don't patronize me." Mrs. Maxmillan's eyes were narrowed and glaring at her husband.

"You asked." He pivoted and threw over his shoulder. "If you have questions for me, Detective, I'll be down in the bar."

Ryan didn't stop him. He wanted to ask the man's wife a few questions about her husband.

"Mrs. Maxmillan, you knew about your husband and the deceased Emma Wickes' relationship, didn't you?"

The woman had dumped every cosmetic bag upside down, pouring the contents onto her bed. "I've known about all of Tabor's obsessions."

Ryan raised an eyebrow. "Is that what you call his affair with Ms. Wickes? An obsession?"

The woman threw her hands in the air and sat on the bed, making all the cosmetic items bounce and roll toward her. "Yes. She was the only woman he couldn't be threatened away from." She looked at her manicured nails. "I bought off every single woman he had an affair with. But Emma…she was in love." The woman said the word as if made her ill. "She was a chorus girl before Tabor made her his assistant. I should have known something was up when he did that. But I thought it would give me a chance to tear them apart, her working so closely with him and my being able to come between them every chance I had." She shook her head. "It only seemed to make them closer. I finally told him to fire her or I'd see to it she spent the rest of her years in jail."

"How would you have done that?" Ryan asked, thinking the woman had enough hatred for the victim to have killed her. The act with the missing jar could be just that, an act to make him think someone stole it.

"Lance would have placed evidence of an illegal activity then sent an anonymous phone call sending the police to her place." She smiled. "The thought of the things he told me he could do were what kept me believing she couldn't steal my husband."

"I heard your husband has been seeking a divorce. Did you know that?" Ryan wondered if Maxmillan had been bluffing on that part.

She sneered. "Yes. Lance discovered my dear husband was working with a lawyer who I battled with years ago. She was the only one who would dare go against me."

This woman had an omnipotent belief in herself and how people perceived her. "Then you knew about the divorce and that Ms. Wickes was pregnant with your husband's child?"

Her eyes flashed with hatred, and her mouth pinched in a rage filled smile. "I knew she had given him what I couldn't. An heir. I offered to pay her a million dollars to hand the baby over to Tabor and I when it was born. She said she would rather die than have their child be raised by me." Her head and hands shook. Mrs. Maxmillan reminded him of the octopus villain in a children's movie he'd watched with his nieces several years ago. If a person's eyes could turn red, hers would have. Her face was crimson. "That insolent bitch would rather die than have me get my hands on her love child. Well, the last laugh is on her. She and that brat are dead. Tabor will come back to me. He always does."

The woman's anger pulsed through the room. He could see her coldly scheming how to kill her husband's lover and child. But he couldn't see her getting her hands dirty to do it. No, it would have been Lance who administered the lethal cream. But how? He needed to talk to all the people who were in the spa area the day of the homicide.

"Thank you for your time. If that missing jar of cream appears, please let me know." Ryan flipped his notebook closed and pivoted to leave the room and penthouse.

"You think it's me because she was allergic to bee stings. Well, it wasn't me, but the thought had crossed my mind more than once." Her voice trailed him out into the hallway.

Ryan stepped up to the elevator and hit the down button. He'd bet his last ten years pay that what Shandra saw in her dream was a man putting cream on the victim's back. And he was going to prove it was Lance Springer.

Chapter Twenty-one

Opening her phone to call Miranda, Shandra noticed the text from Ted with his cousin's number. She aborted the idea to visit with Miranda about Lil's date at Rigatoni's the night before and touched Ted's cousin, Rachel's, number.

"Hello?" a woman answered.

"Hi, Rachel?"

"Yes?"

"You don't know me, I'm a friend of your cousin Ted. I'm Shandra Higheagle and—"

"The potter who makes the gorgeous vases Ted and Naomi have in their gallery?" the woman interrupted.

"Yes, that's me. Thank you for thinking my vases are gorgeous." Even after selling as many vases as she had for amazing amounts of money, she still found it hard to believe people loved her work as much as she did.

"I love your stuff. Especially the ones with the

cutouts. There is something spiritual about them." The awe in Rachel's voice humbled Shandra.

"Thank you again. Those were made at a time in my life when I was seeking my heritage and myself." Learning her Nez Perce family wanted her in their lives had been a shock and exactly what she was needing at the time of their reaching out to her.

"I'm sure you didn't call me to talk about your work. I have to leave in fifteen minutes to pick up my daughter from kindergarten, why did you call?"

"Ted told me you were friends with Emma Wickes."

"It's so sad. I don't know how her parents are able to cope having lost Rory and now Emma. I'd be devastated if both my children died before me." The sorrow in Rachel's voice mirrored the feelings swirling inside of Shandra.

"Did you and Emma keep in touch after she left?" Shandra didn't want the woman running off to get her daughter and not talk about the reason for the call.

"At first. Then she stopped calling and eventually my texts went unanswered." A sadness veiled her words.

"And you didn't know she was here visiting?" Shandra asked.

There was silence. Emma *had* reached out to her old friend.

"I had a feeling she was coming back. But not to see her parents. She didn't ask me about them when she called. And when I mentioned them, she would change the subject."

"They didn't have a good relationship?" Shandra asked, wondering if smothering a child was as detrimental as ignoring them.

"Not after Rory died. Kind of hard for her to have a normal life with her mother always lurking in the shadows. I know Mrs. Wickes said some hurtful things when Emma left. And I think some of what she said became the truth and that's why Emma stopped calling me."

"What are your thoughts on why she came to Huckleberry?"

A deep sigh whistled through the phone. "She asked if Huckleberry had finally moved into the twenty-first century and had a doctor. Then she asked about the lodge. I told her Valerie worked there."

Shandra stared at Sheba as she walked into the kitchen. "Emma knew that Valerie worked at the lodge. Do you think Emma tried to connect with her cousin?"

"I can't say. The two of them never really got along. Emma was good at whatever she set her mind to. Valerie was always trying, but she didn't have the coordination or the self confidence that Emma had." Rachel made a sound. "I really have to go. The teachers don't like it when parents don't pick their kids up on time."

"Thank you for your time. Can I call again if I have any more questions?"

"Any time! Bye."

Shandra placed her phone on the counter. Was Valerie hiding the fact she knew her cousin was in the county and staying at the lodge? Why did Emma want to know about a doctor? She smiled. Ryan could find out.

She texted her husband. *I talked to Rachel. New information. Want to meet for dinner?*

You aren't a detective. He reprimanded. *Meet me at Rigatoni's at 6.*

She smiled. The first sentence was his obligatory nod that she shouldn't be messing around in his case. The dinner invite was to learn what she knew.

Gliding a finger across the front of her phone, she tapped the contacts and dialed Miranda.

"Shandra! I've wanted to talk to you. Did you know that Ruthie and Maxwell are pregnant?" Her friend answered in her usual bubbly tone.

"I just found out. How do you know?" She was sure Ruthie hadn't told her, to spare any hard feelings.

"Alex told me. Ruthie fainted and Maxwell took her to the clinic. She's been going to a doctor in Warner. I guess it would feel awkward to have someone you socialize with to… you know." The embarrassment in her voice had Shandra nodding.

If she were in need of a doctor for gynecological reasons, she wouldn't go to Alex. It would be weird to have her friend's husband seeing that much of her.

"Was Ruthie all right?" Shandra asked.

"She needs to get more water and iron and rest, Alex said. Nothing that threatened the baby." Her relief was palpable.

"That's good. How are you doing? Knowing Ruthie is having a baby?"

Her friends were all in baby mode. While she and Ryan were taking the baby thing slower.

"I'm ecstatic for those two. They have been going together for so long before they married that having a baby so soon is natural." Miranda sighed. "Hopefully, Alex and I can get pregnant soon." She sniffed. "If he can't find a cure, he could only see a few years of his child's life."

Shandra felt for the couple, knowing Alex could become victim to the disease that took his grandfather and father at age fifty-five. "I'm sure if you relax and don't pressure yourselves, things will happen."

"That's what everyone says." Miranda sighed. "You didn't call me to get depressed."

Shandra laughed. "You never depress me. Ryan and I are coming to the restaurant for dinner at six. Will you have a table for us?'

"We always have a table for you. Don't worry." Miranda clanked something.

"What are you doing?"

"Making cookies. I promised Mom I'd bring some for the church auction." Miranda's energy always amazed Shandra.

"Then I should let you go."

"Hey, did you know that Lil and some older guy in a wheelchair were in the restaurant last night?" Miranda kept her on the phone.

"Really? Did they seem to be getting along?" She'd called Miranda to find this out and had forgotten after the other conversation.

"Hey… You knew they were there or you wouldn't ask about if they got along."

"Lil came home in a snit last night. Seems her date left her after Claude from the feed store called her crazy."

"Is that what happened? I just saw Harvey wheeling out and Lil looking dejected. Before I could get over to see what was wrong, she threw money on the table and left."

"She paid for the meal?" Shandra was beginning to

like this Harvey less and less.

"Yes. I think mainly because Harvey left so abruptly, he didn't pay."

"Or he left abruptly to not have to pay." Shandra had listened to enough of Ryan's cases to have become cynical.

"Do you think so? I know he has been in the restaurant before with other people, but I can't remember who paid."

"Other people? Women like Lil or men or perhaps a family?" Shandra was going to dig into this man who hurt Lil and didn't seem to give a person a chance to give their side of the story.

"I think they were all women in their sixties and seventies."

"A gigolo," Shandra said under her breath.

"A what?"

"Never mind. I'll see you tonight." Shandra hung up and went to shower and change to go to town for dinner.

Chapter Twenty-two

Rigatoni's, as usual, for a Friday night was crowded. True to her word, Miranda led them to a table near the kitchen that Shandra knew was always kept open for friends who wandered in on busy nights.

Once they were seated and had ordered, Shandra relayed what she'd learned about Lil's date and Emma having contacted her friend.

"I'll go by the clinic tomorrow and ask Alex if he saw Miss Wickes. But it's odd he didn't say anything when he saw the body." Ryan picked up his glass of iced tea.

"Valerie was family and she didn't recognize Emma when we found her." Shandra didn't like to think about the hives and how Emma must have suffered.

Ryan nodded. "I had a talk with Marcia Maxmillan today."

Shandra leaned toward him. "Was she as intimidating as her husband thinks?" She had yet to visit with the woman. What she'd learned and seen on her own, she knew Marcia wouldn't have the time of day for her. Unless she thought it would benefit her.

"She does try to run everyone."

"Including you?" Shandra knew her husband wouldn't allow anyone to manipulate him.

"Yes. She had enough anger to kill the victim and the child in her. Mrs. Maxmillan loathed the deceased and had an unhealthy anger toward Miss Wickes for defying her twice."

"Wow! Emma had the strength to stand up to Marcia twice?" Shandra leaned back as Miranda delivered their dinners. "Thank you."

"You're welcome." Miranda didn't hurry away, she lingered at the table, twisting the ends of colorful fabric tied around her waist in her hands. "I dropped the cookies off at the church on my way to work and was surprised to see Harvey there. He was helping Mrs. Otterman put the cookies in boxes. They were laughing and having a good time, like I saw him and Lil doing last night."

Shandra's attention was on her friend. "And?"

"Well, I asked around. Since Harvey appeared in Huckleberry, he's been friending older women. Several were only too happy to tell me how they always ended up paying for meals out, using their vehicles to take drives, and sometimes buying him things he says he can't afford."

"He's a scam artist," Ryan interjected.

Shandra had to agree. Lil was better off to forget him.

"I'm thinking he is. Lil should be grateful Claude said what he did." Miranda released the belt she'd been twisting. "Sorry to ruin your dinner, but I thought you should know and tell Lil."

"Thanks Miranda. I'll let her know." Shandra wondered if Lil would even listen.

"I wonder if Cathleen came up with any priors?" Ryan picked up his knife and cut into his steak.

"Then you did have her look into him?" Warmth enveloped Shandra's chest. She should have known Ryan wouldn't let Lil down.

"Yeah. Figured it couldn't hurt."

Shandra swirled pasta onto her fork. "It wouldn't hurt to tell Chief Marlow about him."

Ryan nodded as he chewed.

Picking up her glass for a drink, Shandra caught a glimpse of one of the men that had been in the lodge bar the other night. "Isn't that the man you said was an FBI agent?" she asked, tipping her glass in the direction Miranda had taken the man.

"Where?" Ryan scooted around the curved bench seat to sit next to her.

Shandra's eyes widened. "There. Sitting with Valerie."

Ryan couldn't believe his eyes. What was Trower doing talking to the victim's cousin?

"Maybe they're having a date?"

He looked at his wife. She didn't believe it any more than he did. "They're talking too earnest." Ryan put his cloth napkin on the table and motioned for Shandra to let him out.

She stood. "Do you want me to go with you?" Her tone held interest.

"No. I think I'd rather make this an official encounter." He walked over to the table where Trower and Valerie sat, going slow to hear a bit of the conversation before he showed himself.

"What do you mean Emma told you everything?" Valerie asked.

"I know she came here specifically to see you. Why?" Trower was using an interrogation tone.

"I didn't know she was in Huckleberry until I saw her at the coffee shop." Valerie's voice rose an octave. "I thought you wanted to talk about Emma as a friend. Not accuse me of—of—"

Ryan took this moment to make his presence known. "Trower, what are you doing?"

Valerie's gaze latched onto Ryan with gratitude shining in their depths.

"Greer. Are you following Valerie?" The man glanced at the woman.

"I was having dinner with my wife when I spotted the two of you. I thought it strange for you to be dating so soon after a woman you claim to have loved died of unusual circumstances." Ryan grabbed an empty chair at the table and sat beside Valerie.

Trower's ears blossomed into a deep red. His jaw wiggled back and forth slightly as he ground his teeth. The sound of enamel gnashing enamel could be heard in the confines of the small table.

Valerie stared at the FBI agent. "Were you the married man she was crying over?"

Ryan studied the woman. She hadn't a clue who her cousin was seeing. He was beginning to think Shandra was right about her not knowing a thing about her cousin and having no reason to harm her. "No, he isn't the married man. Just the jilted man."

Trower glared at him.

A waitress arrived with their food. She studied each one as she placed their plates in front of them. She glanced at Ryan. "Would you like to order?"

"No, I'm just visiting," Ryan said, catching a glimpse of Shandra sliding out of the booth they'd shared. "And I need to get back to my table." He stood and glanced at the two. "I'll need to speak to you again tomorrow," he said to Valerie.

Facing Trower, he said, "You I'll talk to when I finish dinner."

Chapter Twenty-three

Ryan ate dinner so fast his meal sat in his stomach like a large rock. He'd wanted to get Shandra on her way home before he questioned Trower about Lance Springer and his movements.

He watched Shandra get in her Jeep and drive down the street before he pivoted and strode between the tables to the one where Trower still sat. The chairs across from him were empty.

"Did Valerie leave?" Ryan asked when Trower glanced up.

"Yes, pretty much as soon as you did." The man stabbed his fork into Shandra's favorite dessert.

Ryan waved down a waitress. "Could you put a slice of tiramisu in a box for me to take home?" He'd go home bearing a gift and maybe be forgiven for rushing her out of the restaurant.

"Why did you want to see me?" the FBI agent asked, picking up what looked like a mixed drink.

"What can you tell me about Lance Springer? Specifically, his movements since he arrived in Huckleberry." Ryan pulled out his notepad.

The waitress returned with the box and a glass of iced tea for him.

"Thank you. That was quick and thoughtful." He picked up the glass of tea.

"Miranda had the dessert already boxed and handed me the iced tea." The waitress spun on her heel and headed to take an order at another table.

He should have known Shandra's friend would have his back. A quick glance found the woman watching him. He raised the glass and mimed, "Thank you."

She smiled, nodded, and went back to work.

"Since you were keeping tabs on Ms. Wickes and anyone else involved with her, I would assume you knew the whereabouts of Springer and the Maxmillans." He poised his pen over the notepad.

"I was only one person." Trower wasn't going to make this easy.

"Do you think Springer had enough time alone in the spa area to have come across Ms. Wickes and applied a cream to her?"

The man's eyes widened slightly before his nostrils flared. "Do you believe Springer killed Emma?"

"I don't know for sure. I do know that Mrs. Maxmillan has facial cream in her possession that has bee venom in the ingredients. And when I asked her about it, she said one of the jars was missing." Ryan continued to study the man. While his anger was justified, the gleam in his eyes was cool, almost calculating.

"You believe Marcia gave Lance a jar of the cream to kill Emma." The agent nodded his head. "It makes sense. If Tabor had decided to finally divorce Marcia and marry Emma, she would have wanted to get rid of the woman taking away her trophy husband and all his money."

Before Ryan could get Trower back on the events at the spa, the agent asked, "Where did Marcia get the cream from? Do you think she brought it with her just to kill Emma?"

The questions were legitimate, but there was something in the way he asked that had Ryan wishing he'd not said anything to Trower. He knew from past experience the agent wasn't always ethical and shouldn't be treating Trower like a fellow cop. The FBI Agent's actions made Ryan wish he'd said less to the man and treated him like the other suspects.

"I'm more interested in knowing more about what you saw Lance doing while he was in the spa area."

Trower studied him. "He came through the employee door that I found locked. Either someone let him in or he picked it."

"Where did he go?"

"He walked down the hall peeking in the rooms. I backed into the lounge and sat down, holding a magazine up so he couldn't see who I was."

"Did you follow after he left the room?"

"I tried. He had disappeared. Then one of the staff told me to wait in the men's area." Trower took a sip of his drink and added, "Lance wasn't in there. Only two older men arguing about sports."

"Do you think Lance could have gotten close enough to Emma to put the cream on her?" Ryan didn't think the woman had been one to allow any man to touch her. From what he'd gathered of her so far, she would have wondered at his being in the spa, let alone singling her out.

Trower shook his head. "I doubt it. From remarks she'd made, she didn't like the guy."

Ryan shoved out of the chair and picked up the dessert box. "Let me know if you think of anything else."

"You didn't answer my questions." Trower rose half out of his chair.

"I don't have to. I'm the investigating officer, you aren't." Ryan strode out of the restaurant. He climbed into his SUV and headed home. Something was niggling at him, but he couldn't pull the pieces together.

~*~

Shandra drove straight home a tiny bit upset that Ryan had dismissed her so quickly after he wolfed down his meal. He was investigating a homicide. It had been plain that he'd wanted to talk to the FBI Agent alone. She hoped he still didn't believe Valerie had anything to do with her cousin's murder.

The lights were on in the house and at the barn. Lil knew how to make coming home feel like home. It saddened Shandra to think Lil might have had a chance at happiness with someone if the old coot hadn't turned out to be a gigolo. Thinking about what Miranda had told her, Shandra wanted to tell Lil what she'd learned right away.

Lil walked out of her room in the barn and headed for the barn doors.

"Do you have a moment to come in the house and have tea with me?" Shandra asked, helping close one of the barn doors with Sheba whining and getting in her way.

"I suppose." Lil fell in step beside Shandra.

She didn't say anything until they were both seated at the counter with a mug of steaming tea in front of them.

"Miranda—"

"Did you go ask her what happened last night? You know I don't like no one gettin' in my business." Lil shoved away from the counter and off the bar stool.

Shandra put a hand on her arm. "I didn't go there to ask her about your date." Though she had called her friend earlier in the day. "Miranda was telling me that when she'd dropped cookies off at the church for their annual auction, Harvey was there laughing with another woman." She eased Lil back onto the stool.

"Miranda said she had asked other women about him and they all said, they'd gone out to dinner and ended up paying, took rides with him and he didn't offer to help out with expenses, and he asked some of them to purchase items for him."

Lil's face reddened. Obviously, he'd treated her the same.

"He's a scam artist." Shandra picked up her tea and sipped. With Lil you just gave her the details and left it at that.

Lil picked up her cup and drank. When she replaced the mug, it clanked on the granite counter. Her eyes were narrowed and the corners of her lips turned down.

"Don't go causing trouble, Lil." Shandra had seen that look on her employee before. It was the one that meant someone was going to get an earful of Lil's blistering tongue.

"I ain't goin' nowhere tonight." She slid off the stool and headed to the back door.

"Don't go anywhere tomorrow either until you cool down."

The slamming of the back door was her answer.

Sheba put her big head on Shandra's thigh and whined.

"Yeah, me too. I wouldn't want to be this Harvey when Lil finds him." She sipped her tea and watched for Ryan's headlights.

~*~

Half an hour later, Ryan arrived home. Shandra's heart swelled when she spotted a box from Rigatoni's.

"Did you bring me tiramisu?"

He kissed her cheek and handed her the box. "I figured I owed you since I rushed you out of the restaurant."

She flipped the lid up on the box and spotted writing. *Give me a call. M.* "Did Miranda box this?"

He studied her. "How did you know?"

Shandra pointed to the message. "Did she say what she wanted?"

"Not a clue. I'm going to take a shower."

She nodded and pulled her phone across the counter. Miranda's number was at the top of her recent calls. She tapped the call on the phone and grabbed a spoon while it rang.

"Shandra, you must be eating your dessert," Miranda answered.

"Yes. Why did you want me to call?"

"I thought we should throw a baby shower for Ruthie. We could do it at my house, but you are better with decorating than I am. We could get pink and blue cupcakes, unless you know if it is going to be a boy or a girl?" The excitement in Miranda's voice proved she wasn't upset by their friend's pregnancy.

"That sounds like a great idea." Shandra had no idea what happened at a baby shower but she had a mother-in-law and two sisters-in-law that would be only too happy to tell her. She spooned a bite of the dessert into her mouth and relished the creamy sweetness.

"When do you think would be a good time to have it?" Miranda asked.

"I'll ask Ruthie what her due date is and if they have any idea about the gender. Then we can figure it out from there." Seeing Ruthie tomorrow would give her an excuse to go to town and make sure Lil didn't kill Harvey.

Chapter Twenty-four

Driving his usual sedate speed along County Road 15, Ryan replayed what Shandra had told him about the dream she'd had during the night. It didn't make sense. He could tell Shandra was bothered by the abstractedness of the dream. She'd seen a woman, most likely the victim dancing between three men. That would be Springer, Trower, and Maxmillan, he figured. Two had tried to catch her and the third had shoved her away. The one who shoved her away had to have been Springer, but he didn't understand why or how the man could have put cream on the victim's back. If he showed her that hostility when she was alive, the victim wouldn't have let him near her.

A horn honking behind him made Ryan glance at his speedometer. He was going twenty miles under the speed limit and the road curved a lot in this section. He pulled over at a driveway and let the person in a hurry go on by.

He sat in his SUV rehashing Shandra's dreams. Dancing flowers and a vine, the mother and baby disappearing, a person in a robe rubbing the victim's back, and now this one. He shook his head and put the vehicle in drive, pulling back onto the road.

A mile down the road his phone buzzed. Shiela Rickman.

"Greer."

"If you have a prospect for the fetus in your anaphylactic shock victim and his blood type is B ask him for a DNA swab." Sheila was a busy person and always got to the point.

"I do have two people who could be the father. I'll get those done today and sent your way." He ended the call. At this point he was fairly certain that the father was Maxmillan, but it wouldn't hurt to check Trower's blood type.

He called Sheriff Oldham and filled him in on what he knew so far, excluding Shandra's dreams. If the sheriff's office or even the state police he worked closely with knew he believed in his wife's dreams and had followed them on several of his homicide cases, they would all laugh at him and perhaps demote him to deputy.

He drove through Huckleberry and straight to the lodge. He found Trower in the coffee shop.

"When can I leave?" the FBI agent asked. From the bruising around his eyes and the grayish pallor to his skin, it was clear the man had spent most of the night in the bar drinking.

"What is your blood type?" Ryan asked rather than answer his question. The man was free to leave whenever he wanted. He'd only been hanging around to find out what was going on with the case, and he was on leave from the agency.

Trower stared at him. "My blood type? What do you need that for?"

Ryan just stared at him.

"O. My blood type is O. Why?"

"Establishing the paternity of Ms. Wickes child." Ryan stood. "And you can leave whenever you're through sticking your nose into my investigation."

Ryan strode across the lobby and to the elevator. The lodge was quiet. Rarely did people check out early on a Saturday morning. He hit the button for the penthouse and wondered if he'd be calling too early for the Maxmillan's.

~*~

Lil's truck had roared off down the lane as Shandra finished cleaning up from breakfast. It appeared the woman hadn't calmed down any with a night's sleep. She pitied Harvey when Lil found him. Her employee did not like to be a victim of any kind.

Shandra hurried into her room and changed out of her pajamas. She'd planned to wedge some clay to start a new project, but with Lil headed to town, she'd better follow close behind her.

Sheba whined to go along and Shandra gave in. The dog loved to ride in the back seat of the Jeep, hanging her head out the window.

In town, the first place Shandra drove by was the Daily Donut. Lil's battered red pickup wasn't on the block. She had no idea where Harvey lived or if Lil even knew. The only thing she could do was drive up and down the streets looking for the pickup. She started on the west side and worked her way east.

"I should have known." Shandra said to Sheba. There was Lil's pickup sitting in front of Ruthie's Diner. "Let's see if she's in there having breakfast or interrogating everyone who comes in about Harvey." Shandra parked as close to the front windows of the diner as she could and rolled all the windows down halfway. Luckily it was the time of the year when there were cool breezes and the temperatures were mild.

Shandra entered the diner and found Lil sitting at the counter. Her hunched shoulders had the look of someone who didn't want to be disturbed. She'd lived with Lil long enough to ignore her body gestures.

"I wondered where you ran off to so fast this morning," she said, taking the empty stool next to Lil.

The older woman glared at her and sipped her coffee.

Ruthie walked over with a cup of hot water and a selection of teas in a tray. "Good morning. Were you two meeting in town for breakfast when you live next to one another?"

"No!" Lil said emphatically.

Shandra smiled. "We just happened to end up in the same place." She glanced at the empty space in front of Lil. "Would you like some breakfast?" she asked.

"No." Lil stood, dropped a couple dollars on the counter and strode out of the diner.

"What's wrong with her?" Ruthie asked, picking up the empty coffee cup.

"She found out Harvey is scum, and she wants to let him know she knows." Shandra hoped that was all her friend planned to do.

"That nice old man in a wheelchair? He's come in

here a couple of times and had soup. He couldn't seem to find his wallet, so I told him it was on the house."

Shandra rolled her eyes. "That's the same thing he's done to nearly everyone in town."

"Really? That nice old man?" Ruthie frowned. "I take it Lil was one of the people who took pity on him."

"Yes, and she's not happy about it." Shandra sipped her tea as Ruthie picked up an order and delivered it before returning to the counter to visit.

"When is your baby due and do you know its gender?" She asked as her friend sat on the stool Lil had vacated. The usual brisk morning of meals and coffee klatches were being taken care of by Ruthie's uncle in the kitchen and two high school girls waitressing.

"Why are you so interested?" Ruthie sipped the cup of coffee she'd brought with her.

"Miranda found—"

"I knew going to the clinic the other day would get word back to her." Ruthie's face wrinkled in worry. "Is she upset?"

Shandra smiled. "Quite the opposite. She wants to throw you a baby shower and asked me to find out when you're due and if it's a boy or girl."

Ruthie shook her head and grinned. "I should have known she'd put her friends first. She always has."

"Well?" Shandra nudged.

"Their best guess is middle of March. And I'm not far enough along to know the gender yet. Maxwell and I have talked about it and we're not sure we want to know. That's part of the fun, wondering if it's a girl or a boy. I really don't care as long as it's healthy. My doctor in Warner says I'm a high-risk pregnancy because of my age." She stared at Shandra. "You are too. You and Ryan better decide if you're going to have a child."

Shandra nodded her head. Right now, they didn't think a child was a good thing in their lives. Ryan was in danger a lot and she was still finding her Nez Perce roots. Still exploring her ancestors and trying to figure out what she wanted as a woman.

They talked of having kids, just not now.

"We'll have children when we're ready." She finished her tea. "I need to go find Lil before she is thrown in jail for assault."

Ruthie laughed and wandered into the kitchen.

Chapter Twenty-five

The penthouse was as perfect as it had been on Ryan's first visit. The occupants, however, were not as hospitable.

"Why are you harassing us again?" Mrs. Maxmillan asked.

"I'm not harassing, I'm trying to solve a murder." Ryan faced her husband. "What is your blood type?"

Maxmillan narrowed his eyes. "Why?"

"Forensics says the fetus was old enough for them to do a paternity test."

"This is ridiculous. I've already told you that I'm the father of Emma's baby." Maxmillan didn't even look at his wife.

"What is your blood type?"

"B."

Ryan nodded. "Since you are willing to claim the baby, you shouldn't mind giving me a DNA sample."

"Swab away." Maxmillan opened his mouth.

Ryan pulled on rubber gloves and opened the long skinny tube he'd stashed in his pocket. A long-handled cotton swab projected out of the tube. He rubbed the cotton around on the inside of the man's mouth, retracted the swab, and closed the lid. "Thank you."

"Is there anything else either one of you can remember about Tuesday?" Ryan put the tube in his backpack and removed the latex gloves.

"After you discovered I had a missing jar of cream, I remembered coming in from a hike on the mountain Tuesday morning and wondering why there were two glasses sitting on the table there." She pointed to the coffee table in front of the sofa.

"Glasses? As in drink glasses?" Ryan pulled out his notepad. "Did you ask your husband about them?"

He glanced at Maxmillan. His face held a stony, lips sealed expression.

"Did you entertain your bimbo in here Tuesday morning?" Mrs. Maxmillan asked.

Maxmillan turned on his wife. "Emma wasn't a bimbo. I loved her and she loved me. And I still want a divorce. I can't live the rest of my life with a woman I believe killed the woman I loved and my child." He spun on his heel and stalked out of the penthouse.

Mrs. Maxmillan's face was white. She crumpled down onto the sofa. "He's going through with it," she whispered.

"Did you kill your husband's lover and child?" Ryan asked. It was evident she was shaken but with her wits down, she may say something she wouldn't otherwise.

"I'd thought of it, but no. I didn't kill that woman." She half laughed. "I would have given whoever did a reward," she sobered, "until my husband stormed out of here just now."

"Who do you think your husband was having drinks with and talking to on Tuesday morning?" He wasn't going to lose sight of the fact two people had been in this penthouse when Mrs. Maxmillan was away.

"The only person I could think of would be Bailey, his bodyguard for the bimbo." Mrs. Maxmillan's lips twisted into an ugly sneer. "She'd like to get her hands on my husband. She might have her chance now that he believes I'm a murderer."

Bailey Ullrich the other person who was sneaking around the spa. "Thank you." He let himself out of the penthouse and onto the elevator. He punched in the fourth floor. He'd see if Ms. Ullrich was in her room.

~*~

Shandra did another street by street search for Lil and was surprised to see her pickup parked at the feedstore where Claude worked. She parked beside the pickup and pushed through the swinging door into the store part of the building.

Lil and Claude were sitting on a couple of hay bales in the back of the room. They had coffee cups in their hands and were talking in normal tones. Shandra slowly backed out of the building. She didn't want Lil to know she was following her around and at the moment she appeared to have forgotten Harvey or why she'd come to town. That was good.

Shandra decided since she was in town, she'd go by Dimensions and see if Naomi was ready for her new vase. She had it boxed up and in the back of her Jeep.

Parking in front of the gallery, Shandra glanced into the showroom and was surprised to see the person

Lil was hunting. Harvey sat in his wheelchair, admiring a painting. This was the second time she'd seen him in the gallery. She wondered if soft-hearted Naomi had given the man money.

Shandra stepped out of the Jeep. "Stay," she told Sheba who was whining to get out. The dog knew Naomi had dog biscuits just for her. "If they tell me to go around back to unload, you may go in." She patted the dog's wide head sticking through the down window.

The door buzzed as she entered.

Harvey glanced her direction then ducked his head and wheeled his chair toward the back of the gallery.

"Where are you going, Harvey?" she asked, walking faster to catch up to him. She grasped the handles of his wheelchair and put the brake on. She'd wheeled an old friend of her father's around at his retirement home before he passed and knew how they worked.

"Oh, hello. Do I know you?" he asked, acting scatterbrained.

"Of course, you do. Why else would you try to get away without me seeing you?" She walked to stand in front of him. "I'm giving you fair warning. Lil does not like to be trifled with. She is mad and she is looking for you. If you want to keep from being scalded by her tongue and have everyone in the town know you are a mooch, you might want to move to another place to find gullible people."

His eyes widened. "I don't know what you're talking about."

She laughed. "You know perfectly well." She started naming off the older women she knew in the community who were single and ended with, "And telling Ruthie every time you go in the diner you can't find your wallet."

His face grew lighter in color and by the time she finished, his hands were shaking.

Naomi walked over to them. "Shandra, I see you've met one of your admirers. Harvey has come in nearly every day to look at your work."

An alarm went off in Shandra's head. "Really?" She sauntered over to the exhibit of three of her small vases and a taller one on a pedestal. A peek into the small ones revealed they were empty.

She couldn't see into the tall one, but a person, standing, could raise their hand and drop something into it.

Harvey made a noise when she grasped the vase and set it down on the carpeted floor. Inside were pieces of jewelry, a watch, items that when taken to a pawn shop could be used for collateral on money.

She tsked. "Harvey, how dare you use one of my vases to hide your stolen goods."

"What?" Naomi rushed over and glanced into the vase. "I had no idea." Her gaze leveled on the man in the wheelchair. "I can't believe I thought you actually admired Shandra's vases."

"What's going on?" Ted arrived.

"Call the police. We just discovered a thief," Shandra said.

Ms. Ullrich wasn't in her room. Ryan rode the elevator down to the main floor. He glanced toward the coffee shop and didn't find her there. Moving on to the restaurant, he found she wasn't there either. When he didn't find her in the spa, or the bar, he decided to see if the person at the lodge registration desk knew anything.

"She and Mr. Maxmillan were going for a hike, I believe." The young man behind the desk pushed black-rimmed glasses up to the bridge of his nose.

"Any idea where they were hiking?" Ryan picked up a map from the counter. It showed all the trails on the mountain.

"I think I heard them say something about Goat Trail, it's the least traveled, because, well, it's more of a goat trail than the other trails."

Ryan found the trail head just as Shandra drove into the lodge parking lot. She took Sheba out of the Jeep and headed his direction, for what he was sure was a doggie pitstop. He debated with himself whether to get her attention. Finally, he gave in knowing both she and Sheba enjoyed hikes.

"Shandra!" he called.

Her head swiveled and she spotted him. Within seconds, she and Sheba were standing in front of him. "What are you doing out here?" She glanced at the trailhead sign.

"Ms. Ullrich and Maxmillan are hiking this trail. I have some questions for them."

She raised an eyebrow. "You could have lunch and wait for them to come back."

"Is that why you're here? Looking for someone to buy your lunch?" he teased.

"Yes. And I have some information about Harvey."

"Harvey, the gigolo?"

"The one and the same."

He glanced up the trail and back at the lodge. "We could grab something at the coffee bar and keep an eye out for them when they return."

She smiled. "Good, because I don't have on my hiking boots."

He peered at her feet. She had on one of her fancy pairs of cowgirl boots. The falling leaves, rocks, and sticks would have made a mess of the suede leather. "Let's go get lunch."

Chapter Twenty-six

Standing in line waiting to order, Shandra hugged Ryan's arm. She was glad she'd come along when she did and he'd called out to her. She didn't like to think what could have happened had he gone up the trail alone after two of the suspects in his murder investigation.

They purchased coffee, tea, and two sandwiches. Ryan found a table where they could both keep an eye on the front door of the lodge.

"Please tell me Lil didn't get arrested for assault on Harvey," Ryan said, picking up his cup of coffee.

Shandra shook her head and blew on her tea. "He was arrested for theft and fraud."

Ryan stared at her. "Really? And how do you know this?"

"Because I caught him." Before Ryan could get upset, she replayed her morning of following Lil and finding Harvey when she went to deliver her vase.

"A con man in our midst." Ryan chuckled. "Do you think Lil had an inkling and that's why she asked me to check on him or do you think she was really falling for him?"

She shrugged. "Only Lil knows what she was thinking or feeling." Shandra bit her sandwich, chewed, and thought about Ryan wanting to talk to Tabor and Bailey. She swallowed and asked, "What did you learn this morning?"

Ryan sipped his coffee and stared at the door. "I'm not sure. My gut is telling me not one of my suspects has told me the truth. Only the truth as they see it. One points at the other, and I'm just going around in circles. I wish forensics could have said this is what caused the allergy and this is how it was administered."

"But we know it was rubbed on her back," Shandra said. "Because of my dream. I just wish the dreams weren't so cryptic. That I would see the face of the killer and not have to figure out who it could be."

"If it was put on her by the murderer, then it had to be someone she would have let near her." Ryan picked up his sandwich and took a bite.

Shandra thought about the massages she'd had. "Not necessarily. If someone had told her to go into the room and get ready for the massage, she would have been face down on the table and unless the person spoke, she wouldn't even know who was there."

"That means any of my suspects could have done it." Ryan wiped his mouth with a napkin.

"No. Only the ones who were in the spa at the time." She smiled.

"You mean only the ones we know of. Those halls aren't that big and the people who work there should have wondered at people wandering around in street clothes." Ryan raised his chin toward the door. "Here they come."

"If anyone would have seen anything it would have been Mindy. She takes away the used towels and sandals on the women's side and refills the refreshments." Shandra started to clean up her food.

Ryan put a hand on hers. "I'll invite them over, then we'll go look up Mindy.

She smiled and picked up her sandwich, happy she could finish it. Ryan walked over to the two as they entered the lobby. They appeared to be making excuses, but Ryan headed them in her direction. As they walked into the coffee bar area, Shandra shoved the chairs across from her and Ryan out a bit with her foot.

"Have a seat," Ryan said, trying to make the two feel as if they weren't being questioned. "Want something to drink?"

Maxmillan and Ms. Ullrich glared at him.

Ryan smiled. "I'll get you both a cup of coffee."

"Skinny latte," Ms. Ullrich said.

Ryan studied Maxmillan. "Would you like something besides coffee?"

The man shook his head once.

At the counter, Ryan watched Shandra start up a conversation with the two. By the time he returned they were looking a little more at ease.

"You are the artist who made the vase in the lobby?" Ms. Ullrich said with awe in her voice.

"Yes, she is. And at the annual art festival held here in the lodge, her pieces usually bring the highest bid," Ryan said with pride.

Shandra gave him a sideways glance. She didn't

like to brag and even if he said it, she felt it was bragging.

"Do you travel much?" Ms. Ullrich asked, obviously enthralled with Shandra's work.

"I do attend many art shows, and I like to teach pottery to children on reservations and at art shows." Shandra picked up her sandwich.

Ryan knew it was his cue to ask his questions. "Mr. Maxmillan, you left the penthouse earlier, before telling me who you entertained in there on Tuesday morning."

Maxmillan scowled. "That's because it isn't any of your business."

"I'll be the judge of that. I have a homicide investigation to run and I'd like to know where all the people involved were and what they were doing on Tuesday morning and afternoon."

Ms. Ullrich put a hand on Maxmillan's arm. "I was briefing him about what Emma had said and done since arriving at the lodge."

He swung his gaze to Maxmillan. "And you didn't want to tell me this? Maybe because I'd wondered at why you have a body guard for your mistress? Why did you feel the need to have Ms. Ullrich stay with the victim?"

Maxmillan ran a hand over his face. He didn't look at anyone, just stared down at the coffee cup in front of him. "I wanted to make sure she wasn't pulling some scam on me. She'd been with the FBI for two weeks. How was I to know if she really loved me and wanted us to start a life together or was working for the feds." He glanced at Ms. Ullrich and then back at his drink.

"But from my understanding, Ms. Ullrich was with Ms. Wickes even before she went to the FBI."

The man ran a hand through his thick dark hair. "I wanted to make sure she was faithful."

Shandra wiggled next to Ryan. He knew this kind of talk would bring back memories she'd settled.

"What did you talk about Tuesday morning?" Ryan changed the topic.

"I said. What Emma did and said." Ms. Ullrich glared at him.

"What did she do and say?" Ryan held the woman's glare with a steady gaze.

"That she wanted Tabor but wasn't sure if he still loved her. She hoped so because she wanted to have the baby and the two of them share in raising it." She stopped and peered at Maxmillan. "I didn't tell you, but she said if you didn't want her, she was going to raise the baby and file a paternity suit against you. Get what she needed to raise the child and not have to work."

"That can't be true. She didn't take Marcia's money when she tried to buy her off." Maxmillan's anger shifted to confusion and denial.

"Think about it. If you had to support her and the child for eighteen years, that would add up to a lot more than Marcia was offering."

Ryan noted the scheming way Ms. Ullrich put the thought into the man's mind that the woman he'd loved hadn't loved him.

Shandra must have picked up on it as well. She stared at the woman and asked, "Was it Emma's idea or yours to take Tabor to court on a paternity suit?"

Ms. Ullrich stared at Shandra. Her eyes narrowed. "Why would I do a thing like that?"

Shandra nodded toward Maxmillan. "To make him think Emma was a gold-digger. To make you look better."

Maxmillan shifted, easing his body away from Ms. Ullrich. "I can see you coming up with that, not Emma. I'm wondering now if you hadn't been the one to talk her into going to the FBI, hoping I'd fall out of love with her."

Panic flashed in the woman's eyes moments before she swallowed and said, "You didn't know Emma as well as you thought."

"I'm thinking I don't know you as well either." Maxmillan rose. "Excuse me, I need to ask the registration desk to find me another room."

"Why is he getting another room?" Shandra asked.

Before Ryan could answer, Ms. Ullrich said, "Because he doesn't trust his wife to not try and kill him in his sleep." She stood and walked away from the coffee bar.

Ryan stood quickly. "I need to catch up to Maxmillan and ask him a question. I'll meet you at the spa." He'd had a thought watching the woman walk away.

Maxmillan was still at the registration desk. Ryan walked over, catching his attention.

"I have one more question."

The man rolled his eyes. "What is it?"

"When Ms. Ullrich was in the penthouse with you Tuesday morning, did you leave her alone at any time?" It would have been a good time for her to have stolen a jar of the face cream.

The man thought. "No. I don't believe so."

Ryan headed across the lobby.

"Wait." Maxmillan strode over to him. "She did use the bathroom."

Chapter Twenty-seven

Shandra stepped up to the registration desk at the spa as Ryan asked, "What do you mean Mindy is on vacation?"

"She called in the day after the lady was found dead and requested two weeks off for vacation," Chad said.

Grace nodded. "You should have heard Alice!"

"It wasn't a planned vacation that anyone knew about?" Ryan asked.

They both shook their heads.

"Does she have a husband?" Shandra asked.

"No, she's single. And I don't know how she could afford a vacation without pay." Chad answered.

"She's been seeing a guy. I think he's one of the ski instructors here at the lodge," Grace added.

"Do you have a name?" Ryan asked, pulling out his notepad.

"Jason Moore or Moregard or something like that.

I'm sure Meredith will know." The phone rang and Grace answered. "Huckleberry Lodge Spa, this is Grace."

Shandra hadn't noticed anything different about Mindy that day, but something had to have happened for her to go on a vacation the day after the murder.

"Let's go talk to Ms. Dremple and then Meredith," Ryan said, leading her out of the spa. They walked across the lobby to the lodge offices. At the main secretary's office, Ryan asked to see Alice Dremple.

Shandra had yet to meet the woman but from Ryan's comments, she was surprised the woman was in charge of the spa. Ryan's description had been of a woman who wasn't good with people.

A short, robust woman with a shock of bright orange hair walked down the hall toward them. If people thought Lil was eccentric, they should take a look at this woman. She wore a sweeping caftan of fluorescent colors that swirled on a background of yellow.

"Detective Greer, what are you pulling me away from my work for today." The woman didn't hide her animosity at all.

"I wondered if you could tell me more about Mindy taking a vacation and give me her phone number?" Ryan pulled out his notepad, all business.

The woman glanced at Shandra and back to Ryan. "She called in the day after I'd suspended Valerie and requested a two-week vacation. What was I to do? She does a good job and I wanted to keep her happy. We were already one person short and I tried to talk her into waiting until we could find a fill-in."

"She wasn't willing to wait?" Shandra asked.

Alice glared at her. "If she would have been you would see her working, now wouldn't you?"

"Her phone number, please," Ryan said, pulling the woman's attention to him.

"I'm sure Tracy here, could help you with that. I've got work to do." The woman spun around and flounced down the hall.

Ryan faced the secretary. She held up a sticky note with a phone number. "Thank you," he said.

Shandra walked over to the desk. "Tracy, you wouldn't happen to know of the last name or the phone number of a ski instructor named Jason More-something?"

"That would be Jason Morehart. He's working as a hiking guide and maintenance man this time of year." She clicked on her computer and wrote on a sticky note. "That's his phone number, but you should be able to find him working the Pine hiking trail if you wanted to talk to him in person." She smiled at the two of them.

"Thank you!" Shandra said

"Not a problem. Meredith said to help you in any way I could. She wants this murder solved and a press release issued stating the lodge had nothing to do with the woman's demise."

"I think that's a wise decision," Shandra replied as she followed Ryan out of the offices.

"Looks like I'll be going for that hike after all." Ryan walked her over to the Jeep.

Sheba stuck her head out the open window.

"We could go with you," Shandra offered. More worried about Ryan hiking around alone than ruining her boots.

"I don't want to put your boots through the horrors

of mountain hiking," he said, opening the Jeep door.

~*~

Ryan hiked a mile-and-a-half up the Pine trail and found two men working on a steep section of the path. The lack of dirt, and river of small rocks the men were corralling with pointed sticks pounded into the ground, reflected the last rain storm had washed away a part of the trail.

"Jason?" Ryan asked, unsure if one of the men could be Morehart or if he'd delegated this job to the men.

"Yeah?" The lankier of the two faced him.

"I'm Detective Greer with the Weippe County Sheriff's Department. I understand you are Mindy's boyfriend."

"I might not be when she gets back." Morehart wiped a long-sleeved arm across his forehead and pulled a water bottle from the holster hanging on his belt.

"You didn't have any idea she was going on a vacation?" Ryan asked, pulling out his notepad.

The man's gaze dropped to the pad. "She in trouble?"

The other man had stopped working and drank from his water bottle as he listened.

"No. But I'd like to know why she left the day after a homicide was committed in the lodge spa, where she worked."

"She had nothing to do with that lady dying." Morehart screwed the lid back on the water bottle and glared at him.

"I'm not saying she did. But I think she saw something. I think that's why she disappeared on a vacation." Ryan held the man's glare.

The anger quickly turned to concern. "You think she saw something and whoever did that lady in could be after her?"

"I don't know about that, but I do believe she knows something. Do you know where she is?" Ryan studied the younger man's furrowed brow and wide, worried eyes. "If I can talk to her, I can figure out if she is safe or not."

"I don't know." Morehart glanced over his shoulder at the other man. He lowered his voice. "Ever since them Maxmillans came here, people have been stabbing friends in the back to show loyalty to them."

Ryan nodded and pulled out one of his cards. "You can call or text me her location when you are in cell service and alone."

That seemed to appease Morehart. He nodded and tucked the card in his back pocket.

Flipping his notepad closed, Ryan headed back down the trail. As soon as he had cell service he was going to try the phone number the secretary gave him for Mindy.

Chapter Twenty-eight

Shandra drove away from the lodge even though she really wanted to hang out and see who she could start up a conversation with and learn more about the Maxmillans and Mindy.

As she drove through Huckleberry, she recognized Valerie sitting in a booth at Ruthie's.

"Only a few more minutes," she told Sheba and parked across the street from the diner.

Inside the diner, she headed straight for the booth where Valerie sat. "What are you doing here? Shouldn't you be at the spa since they're one person short with Mindy on vacation?"

The woman stared at her. "Mindy didn't go on vacation. She just didn't turn up and that's what Alice said to keep anyone from saying something to the police and bringing more bad publicity to the spa." Valerie waved a hand. "She can't afford losing her job any more than I can. I'm on my lunch break and wanted to get away from all the questions about finding my cousin's body and Alice's glares."

Shandra stared at her friend. "You mean Mindy is missing? Wouldn't her boyfriend have mentioned it to the police?"

She shook her head and stirred a fry in ketchup. "I saw him flirting with that lady my cousin was with."

"When was this?" Shandra couldn't believe how many lives the Maxmillan entourage had wormed their way into.

"The day I came back to work. They were sitting in the coffee bar, close together whispering." She looked up from the red abstract she'd painted on the basket paper with ketchup. "That's the day Mindy didn't show up for work."

"Her boyfriend was flirting with another woman. A woman a good ten or more years older than him when his girlfriend 'took a vacation'." Shandra didn't think Tabor Maxmillan killed Emma. He was in love with her and wanted the baby. She could see Marcia getting rid of her competition. But how did Bailey fit in? Because she apparently did, if she was flirting with Mindy's boyfriend.

"I thought the flirting was odd. The lady is a lot older than Jason. He usually goes for the younger ski bunnies." Valerie finished off the fries. "I have to get back to work."

"I'll pay for your lunch." Shandra waved her friend off.

Ruthie arrived at the table. "Late lunch?"

"Actually, I've already had lunch with Ryan." She grinned. "But I wouldn't mind a caramel sundae. Add it to Valerie's bill. I'm paying."

"Coming right up."

Shandra pulled out her phone and texted Ryan. *Valerie says Bailey and Jason were being chummy the day Mindy disappeared.*

You mean went on vacation. He texted back.

According to Valerie she just didn't show for work and Alice is the one saying she's on vacation.

Her phone rang. She answered,

"When did you talk to Valerie?" Ryan asked.

"Just now. I saw her sitting at Ruthie's and stopped. She doesn't believe the vacation story."

Ryan was breathing heavier than usual.

"Are you hiking to see Jason?" she asked,

"No. I'm hurrying down from seeing him. But now I wonder if I should go back up."

His hesitancy to return up the mountain had her wondering at the conversation he'd had with the ski instructor. "Why go back? Didn't you like what he said?"

"He said all the right things for a boyfriend upset with his girl heading on vacation without him. He even had a concerned expression that the police would be interested in her." Ryan had stopped, she could tell by the silence of thuds and rocks skittering.

"What happened to Mindy?" Shandra asked the universe more than Ryan.

"That's something I need to find out. She could be the key to who murdered Ms. Wickes." The sound of movement continued. "I'm going to call her number and if she doesn't answer have deputies talk to her neighbors. I'll see if I can find out how to get in touch with her family and friends. I'll be home late."

"It sounds like it. See you when you get there."

Shandra slid her finger across the screen on her phone as Ruthie appeared.

"Such an unhappy face for me bringing you one of your favorites," Ruthie said, placing the sundae on the table in front of her.

"Sorry. Things are just getting more complicated about the death at the spa." Shandra picked up a spoon as Ruthie slid into the booth across from her.

"How so?"

"Mindy, I don't even know her last name, who works at the spa—she cleans up and puts out fresh towels and slippers. She's missing. Some say she went on a spur of the moment vacation and others just say she disappeared."

Ruthie shook her head. "I don't think she's done either of those."

Shandra stared at her friend. "How do you know?"

"Her parents were in here yesterday saying they were going on a cruise thanks to Mindy. She'd saved up money and wanted them to have a vacation." She shook her head. "Her parents are leaving next week and they wouldn't go if Mindy wasn't here to take care of their cats and dog."

"What are their names?"

"Wes and Debbie Polk. They live at the edge of town going toward Warner. On the left."

Shandra finished off her sundae. "Thank you. I'm so glad everyone comes in here and visits with you." She stood, handed Ruthie money, and hugged her friend.

"Don't get into trouble with that man of yours," Ruthie said as Shandra walked to the door.

"One more stop," Shandra told Sheba as she

climbed into her Jeep and started it up.

~*~

Ryan pulled up to the Polk residence and shook his head. He should have known his wife would figure out more about Mindy from her friends than he did searching the databases. He patted Sheba on the head as he walked by the Jeep.

At the door, he knocked and waited, wondering what Shandra had already discovered.

A woman in her sixties with dark hair answered the door.

He held up his badge and stated who he was.

"Come in. We already have company," Mrs. Polk said.

He nodded and entered.

Shandra didn't even blush or squirm when she saw him. She just patted the space beside her on the couch.

Ryan reached a hand out to the man reclining in a chair. "Mr. Polk, I'm Weippe County Detective Greer."

The man shook hands and waved a hand to Shandra. "This here's—"

Ryan cut him off. "I know my wife."

The couple glanced at one another.

"We thought you came here as a friend of Mindy's," Mr. Polk accused.

Shandra nodded. "I did. I had no idea my husband was interested."

He glanced at her to see if she was pulling off the lie. Her cheeks were a little duskier than usual.

"What have you told Shandra so far?" Ryan asked.

"Mindy came home after the lady died at the spa and said she didn't know if she could go back to work there. The dead body creeped her out." Mr. Polk's expression sagged into sadness. "Mindy has always been a sensitive girl."

"Then the next day she came home, said she'd decided to use some of her savings to send us on a cruise. A gift for letting her live with us since high school." Mrs. Polk beamed with happiness. "Not that she's a bad girl or hard to clean up after, but it was such a selfless gesture."

"Where is she now?" Ryan asked.

"We thought she was at work until Shandra told us otherwise." Mrs. Polk wrung her hands. "What do you think she's doing?"

"Who are some of her friends?" Ryan pulled out his notepad.

"Valerie from work. Jason, her boyfriend. Dolly, she works in Warner, but lives about ten miles from here. She has a place toward the park out there." Mrs. Polk stood. "Would you like coffee?"

"No, thank you." Ryan wrote the names. "What is Dolly's last name?"

"Starns." Mr. Polk shoved his feet down, making the chair raise to a sitting position. "Do you think Mindy is in trouble?"

"I won't know until I can talk to her." Ryan handed his card to the man. "If she returns have her call me. If she doesn't, please call and let me know where to find her. I believe she is in trouble and I can help." Ryan stood, pulling Shandra up with him.

"Trouble? Like going to jail?" Mrs. Polk asked.

"No. I think she knows something about the woman's death at the spa."

"Oh my!" the woman gasped.

"Please, contact me if she comes home or you talk

to her and find out where she is." Ryan led his wife to the door with Mrs. Polk scurrying behind them.

"I will let you know. I don't want to be like the poor Wickes, losing my children."

Out on the street, Ryan faced Shandra. "Why didn't you tell me about the parents?"

"I'd barely been here five minutes when you arrived." She walked to her Jeep. "Want to ride with me to check out her friend's place?"

He shook his head. "I want you and Sheba to go home and stay there."

"But you are going to go check out Dolly's place? It sounds like a good place for Mindy to hide." Shandra stared at him.

"It does, but I'm sure Jason has already looked there. He would know her friends." Ryan opened the vehicle door. "Go home and leave the detective work to me." He closed the door after she'd slid behind the steering wheel. "Please."

"Keep me informed?"

"Of coursed." He kissed her and walked to his vehicle. After starting the engine, he called the sheriff and requested a deputy meet him at Dolly Starns'.

Chapter Twenty-nine

Ryan waited at the lane to Dolly Starns' place. He wanted to make sure he had a deputy with him when he arrived. It always helped to have someone detain anyone on the premise while he searched.

Deputy Trapp pulled up beside him. "What's the deal?"

"We're looking for Mindy Polk. This is her friend's place. If the friend is on the premise, I'd like you to keep her company while I look around."

Trapp nodded and waited for Ryan to ease into a lane that resembled where Shandra and he lived. Pine trees lined the road with an opening that cradled the small log home and one outbuilding.

He caught movement inside the house as he pulled up. Ryan motioned to Trapp to go around back. The deputy jogged to the back, and Ryan walked up to the front door.

Rapping on the door with his knuckles, he peered

through the small window on the door. The darkness beyond made it hard to see if anyone was in inside.

He pounded with his fist. "Detective Greer with the Weippe County Sheriff's Office. Open the door."

"You can quit trying to get in," Deputy Trapp stood at the end of the porch with a handcuffed young woman.

Ryan recognized her as one of the workers questioned after the death. Mindy.

"Thank you, Deputy Trapp." Ryan tried the door. It was unlocked. "Take the cuffs off her. We'll talk in here."

Ryan waited for the young woman to be freed and walk into the house in front of him. He didn't want to be accused of breaking and entering. It was apparent the woman had been staying here.

"Why are you here?" Mindy asked, plopping onto the couch.

Ryan snagged the nearest straight-backed chair and placed it in front of her. "I'm here because I don't think you're safe."

Her eyes widened, but she clamped her lips tight.

"Mindy, I believe you saw something the day Ms. Wickes died."

Her body jerked once before she drew her knees up to her chest, resting her feet on the edge of the couch cushions, and wrapping her arms around her legs.

"What did you see that day?" Ryan noticed Trapp had pulled out his notepad. He appreciated the man would take notes, seeing the person they were questioning would need all of Ryan's attention to get to the truth.

"The usual. Dirty towels, robes, and flip flops.

People enjoying themselves in the lounge."

Her vagueness only solidified she knew something.

"Who did you talk to?" He paused only a couple of seconds. "Was Alice, the manager, in the back?" Giving her facts he knew might loosen her tongue.

She nodded. "She and Chad think they are fooling people. What he sees in that hot air balloon, I'll never know. But they weren't just talking in the empty massage room." Her nose wrinkled in distaste.

"Did you see Valerie when she came back from lunch?"

"Yes. She asked me if I knew which lockers in the women's locker room weren't being used."

"Did you think that was an odd request?" He studied her as she slowly relaxed.

She shrugged. "No, not really. Valerie said she ran into her cousin and was going to give her a massage. Her cousin needed a place to put her things."

"Did Valerie do this often?"

"No. That's why I didn't question it."

"Did you see anyone walking around in the back in street clothes?"

Her gaze flashed to Trapp and back to him. "No one is allowed in street clothes beyond the lockers."

"Do you enforce that rule?"

"I try."

"That day, the day a woman was murdered, there was someone walking around in street clothes wasn't there?"

She nodded.

"Man or woman?" he asked.

"Both."

It had to be Lance Springer and Bailey Ullrich.

"Did you talk to them?"

"I told them both they had to be in robes or leave and forfeit their treatments."

"What did they say?" He leaned forward.

"The man, growled something about he didn't give a rip and walked on down the hall and out the employee's entrance. I wondered if that was how he got in. The woman went into the locker room. I assumed she was going to change." Her lashes lowered and she didn't look at him during the last sentence.

"You saw her later, didn't you?"

"She asked me to put Valerie's cousin in the massage room. She said it was a surprise." Tears glistened in her eyes as she stared at him. "I didn't know she was going…going…Oh, that poor woman!" She covered her face with her hands and cried.

Trapp stepped by him, offering Mindy a box of tissues.

She ripped out three, blew her nose, and patted the tears on her face.

"Was the woman carrying anything when she went into the room?" Ryan continued the questioning.

"I don't know. I put Valerie's cousin in the room, told her to get on the table, like the woman asked me to do. When I came out of the room, the woman stood in the shadows down the hall. I didn't see her go in, but—"

"Why else would she ask you to put Ms. Wickes in the room."

She nodded.

"The money you gave your parents for a cruise and not going to work. Who bought you off and who threatened you?"

Mindy flinched and hugged her legs tighter to her body. "When I went to work the next day, there was a five by seven brown envelope in my locker. It had twenty thousand dollars in it and a note saying if I was smart, I'd take the money and not say a word to anyone." She dabbed the tissue to her eyes as tears slipped out the corners. "I was scared. I didn't do anything wrong, that I knew of, but I figured out that woman had to have killed Valerie's cousin and I was the only one who knew it. I'm not stupid. I gave half the money to my parents, and Dolly is helping me figure out where to move to so the lady can't find me." She sighed. "Or was. I guess now I'm a witness."

Ryan nodded. "I'd like to take you to the police station to look at photos. We need an I.D. on the woman before we can carry the investigation further."

She released her legs, dropping her feet to the floor, and held out her hands.

"You aren't a suspect. You don't need handcuffs." Ryan stood. "Deputy Trapp, please escort Ms. Polk to the County Station. I think there will be less chance of our suspect knowing she's talking to us if we continue this questioning there."

Trapp nodded. "Ms. Polk." He led her out of the log home.

Ryan followed, locking and closing the door behind him. He had a pretty good notion Mindy would pick Ms. Ullrich from the photos, but he'd make sure there was one of Marcia Maxmillan in the mix.

~*~

"That's wonderful you found Mindy," Shandra said. She had a hunch the young woman would be at her friend's house. "Did she tell you anything?"

"I can't tell you that. I called to see if you could let the Polks know she's safe." Ryan said. "We'll be questioning her about the people she saw in the spa area that day. I don't have to tell you not to let anyone know we have Mindy in for questioning."

"She knows something, doesn't she?" Shandra had hoped the woman could help Ryan with the case, but she also knew that put the woman in danger.

"She does. Call her parents but don't tell them that."

"I won't." Shandra ended the call and looked up the Polks' phone number.

She dialed and listened to the ringing.

"Hello?" Mrs. Polk answered.

"Hi, Mrs. Polk. This is Shandra Higheagle, I was at your house earlier today asking about Mindy."

"Oh, yes! Have you found out anything? Jason is here wondering if we've heard anything."

Shandra's chest squeezed. Was Jason looking for Mindy to make sure she kept quiet or was he genuinely concerned? "Oh? Does he usually come by your place to see Mindy?"

"Sometimes. Do you have news?"

Did she ease this woman's worry and give a possible accomplice in the murder the news they had a witness, or tell her they hadn't learned anything to possibly keep the murderer from fleeing?

"I just wanted to let you know my husband has put the whole sheriff's department on finding your daughter." A small white lie was better than letting on they were closing in on the murderer.

"Thank you. Please let us know as soon as you learn anything."

"I will." Shandra ended that conversation and tried to call Ryan. The phone went straight to voice mail. "Ryan, Jason was at the Polks asking about Mindy when I called. I didn't tell them you had her. If Jason is in cahoots with Bailey, I didn't want him to know you were closing in on them. Call me when you get this."

She paced back and forth in the great room. As soon as they'd arrived home, Sheba had bounded out into the forest behind the house and studio. Her dog had the right idea, maybe a walk in the woods would help her clear her mind and settle her fear for the Polks if Jason became hotheaded wanting answers about Mindy.

Chapter Thirty

Placing the five photos on the table in front of Mindy, Ryan asked, "Are any of these the woman who asked you to escort Ms. Wickes into the massage room?"

Mindy studied the photos closely, pushing them one by one away until only the photo of Bailey Ullrich remained.

"You're sure this is the woman who put on a robe and asked you to put Valerie's cousin in the massage room?"

She nodded. "It was her."

"I'll get a statement to that effect typed up. It will need your signature." Ryan stood. "We'll keep you here for a few hours to make sure you're safe while we gather evidence against her."

Mindy nodded.

Ryan left the interview room and glanced at his phone. Shandra had tried to call him. He listened to the message. "Shit!" He strode down the hall to his sister, Cathleen. "Can you get the recording I just did in the interview room printed out so Mindy can sign it. I have to get a warrant to search Ms. Ullrich's things and make sure Mindy's parents are safe. In fact, dispatch a car to their place and have the deputy check to make sure they are alone and to stay with them."

His older sister raised an eyebrow but flicked the button to send out the dispatch. That was one of the perks of being higher ranking than his older sister. For once in their lives, he could boss her around and she couldn't do a thing about it.

He hit reply on his phone.

"You got my message?" Shandra asked.

"Yes. I'm sending a car to keep an eye on the Polks. Mindy picked out Ms. Ullrich. I'm headed for a warrant. I'll be late coming home tonight."

"I thought as much. Be careful." She ended the call.

He had the D.A. on speed dial. It was after six, but the district attorney wanted this murder solved as badly as Ryan did.

A brief rundown of the facts and D.A. Fragnor agreed to get the warrant to him by the time Ryan arrived at the lodge.

~*~

Settling in for the night, Shandra couldn't shake the idea that they were missing something. When sleep eluded her, she walked into the kitchen and steeped a cup of chamomile tea, hoping it would help. She curled her legs under her on the couch and pulled a fuzzy blanket from the back of the furniture to cover her bare legs. It wasn't cold enough yet to start the fireplace but the nights were getting cooler.

Sheba lumbered out of the bedroom and plopped her big head in Shandra's lap. "I know, when I don't sleep, I keep you up." She stroked the hard, wide space between the dog's floppy ears. "What is it I can't put my finger on?" she asked Sheba, staring into the animal's big brown eyes.

"If Bailey asked Mindy to do something and paid her to keep quiet, she must have killed Emma. But would Bailey have enough strength to hold Emma face down while the venom soaked in?" She closed her eyes and tried to remember the dream with a person in a robe standing next to the body on the massage table. All that came into focus was the fluffy robe and belt cinched around a small waist. No hands, feet, or head to try and figure out if the person was male or female.

She finished the tea and leaned her head back on the couch. Closing her eyes, she slowly drifted off to sleep.

Ella appeared in her dream. "Did Bailey kill Emma?" Shandra asked. Her grandmother's head moved back and forth like a horizontal bobblehead. Shandra's gaze followed Ella's arm as it stretched and pointed. Two men had a hold of a woman's arms. Each pulling her a different direction. "Men? A man killed her?" Shandra glanced back at Grandmother but she was merely a wisp of cloud.

Sheba barked.

Shandra jolted awake, watching the beam of headlights move across the far wall. Ryan was home earlier than she'd expected.

~*~

Two deputies waited at the lobby of the lodge

when Ryan arrived. He motioned for them to follow. They all walked into the elevator and took it to the fourth floor.

Ryan strode up to room 418 and knocked on the door. It was ten o'clock. He doubted Ms. Ullrich was an early to bed kind of person.

"Who's there?" a female voice called out.

"Detective Greer," he called back.

"Shit!" came a loud male whisper from the other side of the door.

"One moment," called Ms. Ullrich.

After several minutes the door opened. Ms. Ullrich wore a shiny, flowing robe and Jason, the ski instructor, sat on the sofa, holding a beer. His hair was a mess, his shirt was on backwards, and his feet were bare.

"I have a warrant to search your rooms." Ryan motioned for the deputy to show the search warrant on an electronic tablet to the woman. "Mr. Morehart, you'll have to step out in the hallway with the other deputy."

"I'll just go." Morehart leaned over as if looking for his shoes.

"I'd prefer you step out into the hall and not take anything with you." Ryan frisked the ski instructor and motioned for Deputy Speaks to escort the man out of the room.

"This is ridiculous. Why would I want Emma dead? She was my job. I'm out of work without her alive." Ms. Ullrich walked toward Ryan.

"Ma'am, stand with the deputy." Ryan didn't have to answer the woman's questions. He was looking for a small jar of face cream with bee venom as a main ingredient. He pulled on latex gloves and started on the right side of the room, remembering Ms. Ullrich's room was the first he'd come across. His gaze and hands scanned any space that would hide a small container. A check under the cushions on the sofa and chair came up empty.

When the room had been checked completely, he moved to the bedroom.

Raising the mattress on the bed, he found a cell phone. A press of the on button and Ms. Wickes photo appeared. The phone Ms. Ullrich said she didn't know about. He put that in an evidence bag and continued his search for the face cream.

The clothes were neatly hung in a closet. He checked all the pockets, toes of shoes, and the two extra handbags. He found a small .38 caliber handgun and ammunition. From earlier checks on her, he knew she had a permit to carry. He pulled the suitcases down from the shelf and looked through those. Nothing.

He moved to the bathroom. There was an assortment of cosmetics on the counter. He picked up what looked like a makeup bag and there in the bag was a jar just like what Mrs. Maxmillan showed him and an epinephrine pen. Either Ms. Ullrich was so arrogant she didn't think anyone would search or she thought hiding the items in plain sight might make them less noticeable. Either way, she should have thrown them away.

Ryan bagged the pen and picked up the face cream up with his thumb on the top and one finger on the bottom. He didn't want to mess up any fingerprints that might be on the jar.

Ms. Ullrich's eyes widened at the sight of the jar in his hand when he walked out into the main room.

"Where did you find that?"

"Where you left it." He motioned to the deputy. "Cuff her."

"That's not mine. I didn't kill her." Ms. Ullrich started to fight. Ryan placed the jar on the side table and helped Deputy Taylor subdue the woman.

"I didn't kill her. Someone is framing me." Ms. Ullrich wasn't hysterical, she was pissed. Her eyes were narrowed slits and her lips were rolled back from her teeth like a snarling dog.

"Taylor, take Ms. Ullrich to the county office. I'll be along shortly to question her." Ryan opened the door for the deputy and woman.

Morehart started toward the pair.

"In here." Ryan ordered the man.

Deputy Speaks made sure Morehart entered the room.

"Why are you hauling Bailey off? She didn't do anything." Morehart stood by the door as if he were going to charge out after the woman.

"Did she tell you she paid your girlfriend to keep quiet about seeing her and doing a favor for her?" Ryan crossed his arms and stared at the younger man.

"What are you talking about?" A stubborn, don't mess with me attitude emerged in Morehart.

"Did you really think Mindy went on a vacation? Or did you know she'd been paid to stay away from work?" Ryan waited while the man flashed through what to reply. His eyes stared straight at Ryan but they were blank as his mind scrambled.

"She didn't go on vacation?"

Ryan laughed caustically. "You know she didn't. You were at her parents' today asking about her. Did

Ms. Ullrich send you over there to see if Mindy had told anyone about her?"

"I don't know what you're talking about." The man's objection wasn't as strong as his former comments.

"Did you know the woman you've been fooling around with killed a person?" Ryan decided a blast with the truth was what this playboy needed.

"Bailey wouldn't kill anyone. She's tough, but that's what I like about her. She doesn't take any shit."

He decided to take another tactic. "Did you know you are her subterfuge?"

"Her what?" Morehart's brow furrowed.

"Subterfuge. Her messing around with you takes the heat off of her because she really has the hots for Tabor Maxmillan and plans to marry him."

"No way! She told me all about him. How hard he is to work for and how badly he treats everyone." Morehart crossed his arms and glared.

"You obviously haven't seen the two together. They spend a lot of time, alone together."

"You're lying!"

A knock on the door and Trower walked in. "What's going on? I saw a deputy escorting Bailey out of the lodge and now this guy's in here yelling so loud I heard him from the elevator."

"Trower, you aren't needed or wanted in here." Ryan motion for Taylor to escort the FBI Agent out of the room.

"Trower?" Morehart started for the agent. "Bailey said you were out to get her."

Ryan grabbed his arms, holding him until the deputy shoved Trower out and closed the door.

"What did Bailey say about Trower?" Ryan asked.

"That he couldn't get over the fact some woman had Maxmillan's baby." Morehart made a sour face. "Who'd want to be tied down by a woman and a baby."

"Help him find his shoes and bring him to Warner, too," Ryan told Speaks as he bagged the jar of face cream.

Chapter Thirty-one

Shandra waited for Ryan to come through the door. When he didn't, she walked to the back door and peered out.

Sheba bounded out into the darkness. The only vehicle under the lean-to was Lil's. Her employee hadn't been here when Shandra came home.

She slipped her feet into a pair of winter boots that sat in the laundry room, pulled the blanket she held tighter around her shoulders, and walked to the back of the barn. Since she wouldn't be able to fall asleep again until she talked to Ryan, she might as well see what Lil had been doing.

At the back door to the barn, Shandra tugged on the leather strap that raised the metal bar on the inside of the door. The door creaked as she pushed it open.

"Who's there?" Lil called out. "I got a shotgun!"

"It's me," Shandra called back, not taking another step for fear her trigger happy friend would shoot.

The door to the room Lil occupied opened. Light flowed out of the small confines giving Shandra a visible path to the room.

"What are you doin' out here this time of night? And without your furry body guard." Lil backed up allowing Shandra into the room.

The moment Lil wasn't in shadow, Shandra took in the way she was dressed. It appeared her friend had been out on a date. She had on a nice suit in a pale lavender and a shirt covered in purple and yellow pansies. Her feet were encased in Lil's favorite pair of purple cowgirl boots.

"I was worrying about Ryan and saw you came home, so I thought I'd come visit." She wasn't about to mention how Lil was dressed or pry into where she'd been. That was the quickest way to make the woman clam up and not say a word.

"He still trying to crack the dead lady at the spa?" Lil sat down on the bed and motioned for Shandra to take the straight-backed wooden chair.

Lil's residence consisted of the twin-size bed, small table with one chair, a dresser, two burner electric cook top, a small refrigerator, a toaster, and electric coffeepot.

"Yes, we thought he'd figured it out, but I'm not so sure." While she and Lil worked alongside one another and over the years had learned more and more about one another, Shandra hadn't told Lil about her dreams.

"Why aren't you sure?" Lil walked over and filled the tea kettle with water from a jug. She placed it on one of the burners.

"It's a feeling. He's talking to a woman but I think it was a man." Shandra didn't know how else to explain her dream and thoughts.

"Why do you think it's a man?" Lil sat back down on the bed after putting tea bags in a ceramic teapot.

"One reason is, why would the victim remain face down on the table if she started reacting to something she was allergic to? I would think she'd try to get help."

Lil nodded. "You think who did it had to be strong enough to hold her down."

"Yes. When someone realizes they could die, adrenaline kicks in, giving them strength they may not have had before."

"That fancy doctor who looks at the dead bodies see anything that showed she'd been held down?" Lil gazed at her with just a touch of superiority.

Shandra held back the smile at Lil's smugness. "I don't know." She pulled her cell phone out of her pajama pocket and texted Ryan. *Were there any bruises or marks from hands holding the body down*?"

"Is that the only reason you think it was a man?" Lil asked.

"If Emma, the woman who died, knew who had walked in the room, I think she would have only remained vulnerable, lying face down on the table for someone she trusted or loved. I don't think she trusted the woman Ryan is talking to. That woman asked another person to lead Emma into the room."

"Who does that leave as someone she'd trust or love?" The kettle whistled and Lil moved to pour the water into the teapot.

"The father of her unborn child, her cousin, Valerie."

"Your friend who you are proving didn't do it." Lil shook her head. "You have to learn, not everyone is a friend even if you call them one."

Shandra stared at Lil. That might be the clue that solved this murder.

~*~

Ms. Ulrich stared straight ahead, not answering any questions. They could only hold her for 72 hours without charging her. While Ryan had found the cream that he was sure caused the victim's death, the victim's phone, and epinephrine pen in the suspect's possession, he had to find a way to make the woman confess. There was no way forensically to say the cream had caused the anaphylactic shock.

He'd also read Shandra's text asking about bruising. He was sure if there had been any marks that indicated a struggle, Sheila would have mentioned it. But Shandra's comment had him wondering what she was thinking. He'd thought about calling her before he started questioning, but didn't want to give the woman any more time to think of ways around the evidence.

Ryan pulled out the signed statement by Mindy and his notes from his interview with Trower. He also had the three bagged items he found in the woman's possession. "I have two witnesses who saw you in the treatment area of the spa on the day Ms. Wickes died."

"I told you I was there." She glared at him.

He nodded. "You did. But you left out the part where you asked one of the workers to put Ms. Wickes in a massage room and then left a packet of money in her locker."

"That little snitch! I did ask her to put Emma in a room and I left the money because I knew you'd think I killed her because of what I'd asked." Ms. Ullrich stared down at the ring that she twisted around and around her finger.

"Didn't you kill her? You had the jar of cream in your cosmetic bag along with the missing epinephrine pen. The victim's phone was found under your mattress." The woman looked shocked at that. "And you paid an employee to not say you asked to have the victim put in a massage room." Ryan studied her.

She tossed what he'd said around behind her downcast eyes. "I didn't kill her." She glanced up, defiance sparking in her eyes. "You can't prove it with the phone, the pen or the cream. I haven't seen that phone since Emma went down for coffee. As for the pen and cream…I haven't touched them and don't know where they came from."

"All three items are enough evidence to hold you and take you to court." Mostly circumstantial, but she didn't need to know that.

"Springer and Trower were lurking in the shadows in the treatment area of the spa. Have you brought them in for questioning?" She stared at him, unflinching.

"But they aren't who you're covering for." Ryan absently flipped through the investigation file. "I'd say, you either killed the victim and her baby to have a chance with Tabor Maxmillan or you and Maxmillan set up the meeting between he and the victim in the spa." He waited a beat. "To kill them both."

Her eyes widened briefly before darkening in anger. "Tabor had nothing to do with the death of Emma. He loved her." The first sentence was filled with conviction, but the second choked her on the way out.

"But you wanted her and the child to go away, just like Mrs. Maxmillan wanted them to go away." He flipped to the pages in the report that had all of Mrs. Maxmillan's comments typed out.

"I would have still been close to Tabor if he'd left Marcia. He told me he would keep me on to be the body guard for Emma and the child." She smiled viciously. "Marcia wouldn't even have been able to come near any of them."

"Why did you steal that jar of cream from the penthouse when you were up there talking business with Maxmillan?" Ryan wanted to confuse her enough she'd slip up.

"I didn't take a jar of cream. When you walked out of my room with it today is the first I've seen of it." She peered in his eyes, no hesitancy or wavering.

"Where did you see Trower and Springer?" he asked.

"Springer had stepped into the back area when one of the employees told him he had to go in the men's locker room and change."

"Where were you?" Ryan asked.

"I'd ducked into the lounge when I heard footsteps."

"Were you spying on Ms. Wickes?"

She scowled. "I knew where she was. I was waiting for someone."

"Maxmillan? Had you called him when you'd discovered Ms. Wickes was in the spa? Was that who you sent to the room where you'd had Mindy escort Ms. Wickes?"

Her body had been straight, but it snapped as if a string had tightened along her spine.

"That's who you are lying for, isn't it?" Ryan spread out the papers with the evidence he would give the district attorney. "All of this says you killed a woman. Does Tabor Maxmillan deserved so much loyalty, you would go to prison for life for a murder he committed?"

She stared at the papers.

"Think about it. He has had lover after lover all while being married to Marcia. She'd allowed him to play however he wanted. I think he used you to help him get rid of a woman who had become a liability. After all, she may say she only wanted him to marry her, but what if she turned out to want everything and held the child over his head to get it?" Ryan pulled out the list of women Catherine had listed that had been linked to Maxmillan. "That's a long list of women he or his wife bought off."

"Tabor only wanted to talk to Emma. He loved her and was excited about the baby. He didn't even go in the room." Ms. Ullrich leaned back in the chair. "That FBI agent was messing around in the hallway when I went to get Tabor at the employee's door. I sent him back out when I saw your wife standing at the door like a damn guard dog."

Ryan shoved the papers into the folder. "Did you see Trower after that?"

Ms. Ullrich shook her head. "It was like he'd disappeared."

"You'll have to stay here until I check more things out." Ryan left the room and instructed the female deputy to take the suspect to a holding cell. He went down to the breakroom where he'd left Mindy.

The young woman sat curled on a chair, staring into the cup she held in her hands. She glanced up at his approach.

"I just talked with Ms. Ullrich. She admitted she gave you the money to keep you from saying she'd asked you to bring Ms. Wickes to the massage room."

Mindy sighed. "Do I have to give the money back?"

"I think you keeping it is a good way to show her she can't buy her way out of things."

Mindy smiled. "Thank you."

"I have a couple more questions. Do you remember seeing a tall thin man with a brown crew cut wandering around in the treatment area?"

She thought then smiled. "Yes. I bumped into him twice. The first time he asked me about all the rooms, and the second time he was wiping his hands on a towel and shoved it into the hamper of dirty towels I had gathered."

"Where did he go?" Ryan had a feeling he'd found his murderer.

Chapter Thirty-two

After a long talk on the phone with the district attorney, Ryan had headed home. With Ms. Ullrich in custody, Mindy tucked away in a motel in Warner, and Morehart also being held overnight as an accomplice, Trower wouldn't get wind the investigation had changed course.

It was two in the morning as he slipped into bed, trying not to disturb Shandra. He wiggled under the covers and closed his eyes.

The light flashed on and cold air swirled around him.

Opening one eye, he focused on his wife, sitting against the headboard staring at him.

"I think you have the wrong person," she said.

He pulled himself up to sit with his back against the headboard. "And who do you think I should question?"

"The FBI agent. I think it was someone she trusted

enough to remain face down on the table as she talked. You mentioned he'd become close friends with Emma. And something Lil said tonight. 'Not everyone is a friend even if you call them one.'"

He nodded. "I have forensics checking for fingerprints on the jar of face cream and epinephrine pen I found in Ms. Ullrich's cosmetic bag. And Ms. Wickes phone, I found in Ms. Ullrich's room. Mindy can place Trower in the back area before the time of death and walking away quickly wiping his hands on a towel, after the time of death."

Shandra spun toward him. "I knew it!"

He held up a hand. "Proving it is another thing. But the D.A. and I cooked up a plan tonight." He kissed her. "Go to sleep."

Ryan slipped back under the covers as the light went out. With luck and the man falling for the trap, they'd have the killer behind bars tomorrow.

~*~

After Ryan and D.A. Fragnor ran through the plan with Mindy, they decided the best place for her to wait for Trower to take the bait would be her friend's place on the way to Warner. It would be the logical place for her to hideout and if Trower used his training, he'd have discovered the friend.

What they couldn't agree on was having someone in the home with Mindy other than her friend. The friend thus far had been kept out of everything. Shandra had offered to help anyway she could, but Trower knew she was married to a cop.

They decided the new young female deputy would stay at the house with Mindy for support and to help apprehend the suspect.

Mindy made the call, telling Trower she knew he'd gone in the room with the dead woman and had been wiping his hands as he left. She asked for ten thousand dollars and wanted it delivered to her at her friend's house before four or she was going to tell the police.

Ryan wished they could just arrest him when he arrived, but they needed him to say he'd killed Ms. Wickes. For that, he wished Shandra could be at the house. She had a way of making people talk. He feared Mindy would get scared when the man arrived and not be able to draw the information out of him before he dropped off the money and left. Or tried to kill her. That was Ryan's worst fear. She'd agreed to help, hoping to absolve herself of leading the victim to her death. At least that was how Mindy saw it.

He drove Mindy to the house along with the female deputy.

"Just hang out, watch T.V. or play cards. We'll be setting up the listening devices while deputies spread out around the house in the trees." Ryan and a State Police technician placed a listening device in all the rooms, uncertain what Trower might try.

"I'd feel better if you were in the house, too," Mindy said as Ryan started to leave with the technician.

"I'll be in a van hidden in the trees, listening." He stepped out the door and discovered his wife arguing with Deputy Speaks.

"What are you doing here?" Ryan asked, striding up to the two.

Shandra whipped around to face him. "I know you said Trower will remember I'm your wife, but I don't believe Mindy can get the information out of him like I can." She peered into his eyes.

He knew what she meant. She had the information from her dreams that she could question Trower about. Ryan shook his head. "I haven't cleared your participation in this with the district attorney. And I'm pretty sure he'd say no."

"But what do you think?" she asked quietly.

"Doesn't matter what I think. It's the D.A.'s call, not mine." Ryan grasped her arm, leading her to the Jeep. At the vehicle he said, "Go home. I know you could get the information out of him better than Mindy, but we can't take the chance he'll see you and know it's a set-up. Go home. Please."

She studied him. "Do you think Mindy could memorize three things to ask him?"

"What do you mean?"

"There are three things that she could say that might help the investigation."

Ryan studied her. "This have to do with the dreams?"

She nodded.

"Write them down. I'll have both Mindy and Deputy Sloan memorize them."

Shandra pulled a piece of paper out of her pocket. "I figured you wouldn't let me in." She kissed his cheek and sped down the road.

Grinning he opened the paper and read the questions.

How did you feel when you realized Emma was having Tabor's baby?

Who did you want to hurt more? Tabor or Emma?

Did you walk into that room pretending to be a friend when all you wanted to do was take her life and the baby's?

Ryan had to admit, Shandra had gone straight to the core of the reason behind the murder. He walked back to the house, knocked on the door, and waited for Deputy Sloan to answer.

Once inside, he showed the paper to the two women. "I want you to both memorize these questions and if Mindy doesn't remember to ask one, Sloan, you being her best friend can ask. It would be assumed Mindy had confided in you about the whole thing."

The deputy nodded.

Mindy stared at the questions. Finally, she glanced at him. "You think he took her life over jealousy?" The surprise in her voice wasn't lost on Ryan.

"It is one of the oldest reasons for murder." He studied them both and scanned the room. They'd been playing a game of cards. The clock said it was three. "I'll be out in the van. He could be showing up any time." Ryan left out the back door and walked into the woods behind the house. He climbed into the surveillance van they'd borrowed from the State Police for this operation.

"This is a big-time operation," Joey Flood, the technician on borrow from the State Police, said.

"You mean for Boondocks Idaho?" Ryan had to admit, this was the first time he'd conducted a sting of this type since becoming a detective with the Weippe County Sheriff's department. He'd been in on plenty of them working undercover in Chicago five years ago.

The technician laughed. "Yeah."

A radio crackled. "Vehicle approaching."

"Anyone have a visual?" Ryan asked.

"Affirmative. Looks like our guy," Deputy Speaks replied.

"Everyone stay put until I give the word." Ryan motioned to Flood. "Turn up the sound in the house."

The two women weren't saying much, but he could hear the rapid slap of card as someone shuffled.

A knock on the door.

A whispered curse and footsteps.

"Hello?" Deputy Sloan answered the door.

"Who the hell are you?" Trower growled.

"Dolly Starns. Who are you?" she said with as much animosity as Trower had tossed at her.

"Where's Mindy?"

"Hey!"

Ryan pictured Trower pushing his way into the house. He got on the radio. "Anyone see if he was carrying?"

"Negative. Couldn't see from my vantage."

"Also couldn't see."

"Not sure."

Damn! Ryan pressed the earphones tighter to his ears.

"You think I'm going to pay you because you saw me in the spa? Well you have another thing coming if that's what you think." Trower's voice was more forceful than Ryan had ever heard it.

"Is this how angry you felt when you realized Emma was having Mr. Maxmillan's baby?" Mindy asked.

Ryan was proud of how her voice didn't shake.

"What do you know about Emma and a baby?" Doubt inflected Trower's tone.

"Valerie was Emma's cousin. She's also my friend. She told me everything that Emma told her about Mr. Maxmillan, the baby…" she paused. "And you."

"Me? What the hell did she say about me?" His voice rose in timbre.

"That you had thrown yourself at her and she'd rejected you. Did you kill her to get back at Emma or Mr. Maxmillan because he had her love?" Mindy's voice faltered just a bit that time.

The tall man turning his anger on the slight Mindy had to be nerve wracking for the young woman. Ryan wished he had enough on the man to take him in without him divulging the deed.

"He didn't have her love! I had her love. She was infatuated with the man because of his money and his charm. But she didn't love him."

"Sounds like you're trying to convince yourself," Deputy Sloan said.

"What the hell do you know? I talked her into testifying against him. I even had her talked into getting an abortion. Told her she didn't need the remembrance of that selfish man around. I took her to a doctor." A loud crashing sound and a squeak from one of the women. Probably Mindy.

"She was still pregnant when she died," Sloan said matter-of-factly.

Another crash. "She snuck out of the doctor's office and straight to Maxmillan. He threatened to tell the F.B.I. about how I'd coerced an informant into taking a life if I didn't leave Emma alone."

"But he saw you at the lodge. Why didn't he do anything?" Mindy asked, her innocence and curiosity shining in her voice.

"Because he didn't think I'd have the balls to cause a scene with him around." Trower laughed. Not the laugh of a sane person, but the cackle of someone coming unhinged.

"Did Emma think you were still a friend when you walked into the massage room?" Mindy asked.

"She glanced over her shoulder, saw me, and started to get up. I told her I was there to apologize. She relaxed, I started rubbing her back with the cream I'd taken from Marcia. I'd planned to frame her, but when Bailey saw me outside the room, I decided, I'd turn the tables on her."

"What cream?" Mindy asked.

"Face cream with bee venom. It works wonders on old wrinkly faces and to kill someone allergic to bees."

Ryan gave the signal for the deputies to storm the house. They had what they needed to start building a case against Trower.

"I'm surprised you're telling us all of this," Sloan said.

Another cackle from Trower. "You won't be around to tell anyone."

A gun shot rang out.

Ryan hit the door of the van and raced to the house. He ran through the back door behind Deputy Trapp.

Deputy Sloan stood over Trower, her Glock pointed at him. Mindy was curled in a ball on the couch. Blood trickled from the arm Trower held.

"Nice job, Sloan," Ryan said, before walking over to Mindy. "Are you okay?"

She nodded. "Did we get him to say enough?"

"You did great. Come on. I'll take you home."

Chapter Thirty-three

The smell of garlic, tomatoes, and cheese made Shandra's stomach growl. Tabor Maxmillan had invited she and Ryan to Rigatoni's along with Valerie, Mindy, and Emma's parents. They had a large table at the back of the establishment. Tabor must have paid to have the tables around them remain empty while they dined.

"I wish I was meeting you as a perspective husband for Emma," Tabor said to the Wickes.

"I'm glad she had found love. I would have enjoyed being a grandmother." Mrs. Wickes dabbed at the tears trickling at the corners of her eyes.

"I wanted to be the father of our child more than anything." Tabor glanced down, hiding the tears in his eyes. He drew in a deep breath and raised his head. "This is to be a dinner in honor of Emma and our child. I want only happy thoughts, and I'd love if you'd tell me stories about her."

While Valerie and the Wickes told Tabor about

Emma, Shandra leaned over to Mindy. "I heard you were a big help in getting the information out of the F.B.I. agent."

The young woman's cheeks reddened. "I don't know if I was a help. When Trower pulled a gun, I just about fainted, but the deputy pulled hers from somewhere and shot his arm holding the gun." She grinned. "It was like being in a movie."

Shandra glanced at her husband. It hadn't been a movie to him. He'd thought he'd put the young woman's life at risk.

"Luckily for us, a partial of Trower's prints were found on the jar and the phone. And Ms. Ullrich's testimony he'd been standing by the massage room door minutes before the victim was found dead will work against him. And we found him in the lodge video footage breaking into the penthouse and Ms. Ullrich's room when no one was in the rooms. We have plenty of evidence to convict."

"I'm glad it wasn't Mr. Maxmillan, he's awfully nice." Mindy stared dreamy-eyed at Tabor as he told a story about a trip he and Emma took.

Shandra batted her eyelashes at Ryan. "I think you're awfully nice, too."

"Too? Have you fallen for Maxmillan's charms as well?"

"No. You're the man of my dreams."

~*~

Thank you for reading ***Toxic Trigger-point.*** What inspired this story was a mini-vacation for my husband and I. I'd won a spa package in a silent auction and while lying facedown on a massage table waiting for my masseuse to return to the room, I thought, "What if, I were a dead body and the poor masseuse discovered it when she came in to do her job?" And that my readers is how a writer's brain works. Everything we come upon is potential for a story.

I hope you will continue to follow Shandra and Ryan's investigations as they now work together to solve murders as a married couple. In the next book Shandra is asked to judge an art contest in Kauai, Hawaii. And you know where Shandra goes, there is a murder for her and her grandmother to solve.

If you enjoyed this book, please leave a review. It is the best way to thank an author for an enjoyable read. I love to hear from fans. You can contact me through:

website: www.patyjager.net
Blog: writingintothesunset.net

All my work has Western or Native American elements in them along with hints of humor and engaging characters. My husband and I raise alfalfa hay in rural eastern Oregon. Riding horses and battling rattlesnakes, I not only write the western lifestyle, I live it.

Thank you for purchasing this Windtree Press publication.
For other books of the heart, please visit our website
at www.windtreepress.com.

For questions or more information contact us
at info@windtreepress.com.

Windtree Press
www.windtreepress.com

Hillsboro, OR 97124